PRAISE FOR

A VERY SIMPLE CRIME

"*A Very Simple Crime* is the product of A Very Talented Writer. Grant Jerkins's stylish prose and rich characters set him apart. As a reader, you will enjoy every page. It's impossible this is a first novel. Don't miss it."   —Ridley Pearson,
New York Times bestselling author of *In Harm's Way*

"There's not a soul you can trust in the story . . . [A] well-fashioned but extremely nasty study in abnormal psychology, which dares us to solve a mystery in which none of the normal character cues can be taken at face value."   —*The New York Times Book Review*

"No one in this novel is as [he or she] appear[s] to be, and the twists and turns never let up until the very last page. This dark, chilling debut . . . is a real page-turner and should especially appeal to legal thriller fans."   —*Library Journal* (starred review)

"You have to admire the purity of Jerkins's writing: He's determined to peer into the darkness and tell us exactly what he sees."
—*The Washington Post*

"Beautifully plotted, aware of its genre roots yet wholly original, funny, scary, haunting . . . and oddly arresting from the very first sentence."   —Nicholas Kazan,
playwright and Oscar-nominated screenwriter of *Reversal of Fortune*

"Jerkins juggles his plot twists like a top circus acrobat in this nasty legal noir."   —*Publishers Weekly*

AT THE
END OF
THE ROAD

GRANT JERKINS

BERKLEY PRIME CRIME, NEW YORK

THE BERKLEY PUBLISHING GROUP
Published by the Penguin Group
Penguin Group (USA) Inc.
375 Hudson Street, New York, New York 10014, USA

Penguin Group (Canada), 90 Eglinton Avenue East, Suite 700, Toronto, Ontario M4P 2Y3, Canada
(a division of Pearson Penguin Canada Inc.)
Penguin Books Ltd., 80 Strand, London WC2R 0RL, England
Penguin Group Ireland, 25 St. Stephen's Green, Dublin 2, Ireland (a division of Penguin Books Ltd.)
Penguin Group (Australia), 250 Camberwell Road, Camberwell, Victoria 3124, Australia
(a division of Pearson Australia Group Pty. Ltd.)
Penguin Books India Pvt. Ltd., 11 Community Centre, Panchsheel Park, New Delhi—110 017, India
Penguin Group (NZ), 67 Apollo Drive, Rosedale, Auckland 0632, New Zealand
(a division of Pearson New Zealand Ltd.)
Penguin Books (South Africa) (Pty.) Ltd., 24 Sturdee Avenue, Rosebank, Johannesburg 2196,
South Africa

Penguin Books Ltd., Registered Offices: 80 Strand, London WC2R 0RL, England

This book is an original publication of The Berkley Publishing Group.

FIRST EDITION: November 2011

Library of Congress Cataloging-in-Publication Data

Jerkins, Grant.
   At the end of the road / Grant Jerkins. — 1st ed.
    p.   cm.
   ISBN 978-0-425-24334-3
   1. Life change events—Fiction.   2. Secrets—Fiction.   3. Psychological fiction.   I. Title.
   PS3610.E69A94 2011
   813'.6—dc23   2011028158

PRINTED IN THE UNITED STATES OF AMERICA

10 9 8 7 6 5 4 3 2 1

For my sister,
Amanda Grace Beam

CONTENTS

AT THE
END OF
THE ROAD

GOD IS

He was just a boy.

In her mind, the woman could conjure only a faint static image of the boy, like a photograph faded with time and constant handling.

The woman's room in the Clermont Hotel overlooked Ponce de Leon Avenue. The Clermont, a fading redbrick monolith, wasn't the worst the city of Atlanta had to offer, but it was close. The hotel was noted for its late-night lounge, located in the basement, its main attraction being Blondie, a stripper who crushed beer cans with her breasts.

The woman knew what she had come here to do. Not consciously. She never consciously acknowledged to herself that she had come here to end her life. But that knowledge was there inside her, hidden away. Just as whatever it was that had gotten her to this point existed somewhere deep within her—but she was not allowed (or did not allow herself) to see it. Still, it was there inside her, hard and ugly and shameful.

The woman looked at her reflection in the spotted mirror. Why did men still want her? Why would they pay to have sex with her? What was wrong with men that they would pay to have intercourse with a thirty-seven-year-old meth addict who looked a haggard fifty? And she realized that she had never understood the sex act, what drove men and women to seek it out—in one form or another—over and over throughout their lives.

She finished the last of the tranquilizers, washing them down with water from the bathroom sink. Already she could feel the soothing warm fingers invading her, holding her. This was the only penetrating embrace she had ever cared for. She wished she hadn't finished the vodka beforehand, because now she needed to hurry. Now her conscious mind knew what her other mind had done. Now her two halves were working together, and for the briefest moment the point in her life when she had first been divided flashed in her mind and she saw the hard shameful thing and it didn't hurt because the hard thing was dying now.

She found a soiled Rite Aid receipt stuck to the bottom of the trash can and wrote five words on the back of it. She folded the paper and wrote the boy's name across the front. She tucked the note inside the Xanax bottle, capped it, and put it in her pocket.

And she thought of the boy, and she thought about the hard, ugly, shameful thing deep within her, and she was happy because she realized that she was winning. She was going to kill that thing inside her.

THE
RETICULATED
WOMAN

THE PASSAGE OF SLOW-MOVING TRACTORS had ground the red clay surface of Eden Road into a fine, rust-like powder. And the stern eye of the Georgia sun baked the powder drier than crematory ash. Speeding cars that sometimes used the lonely road as a shortcut to the reservoir left massive, lingering red plumes in their wake.

When the woman's car flipped over, it sent up rolling, choking clouds of the stuff. And now the woman stood in front of the boy, both of them covered in the rust-colored dust. The blood that seeped from the woman's scalp wound etched thin lines down her soiled face. And as the blood spidered through the dirt, it left an obscene red reticulation, a web of gore.

The boy stood, unmoving. His mind could not yet fully process how his environment—an environment that seemed to never change—was, in a matter of seconds, changed with a ferocity that defied comprehension.

The woman stumbled toward the boy, her hands held out

stiffly before her like a zombie, like Frankenstein's monster, and the boy could see that blood also dripped from her fingertips, and he could see through the dirt and the blood that her fingernails had been torn away in the accident, ripped out from their beds, leaving an exposed jangle of nerves and meat.

EDEN ROAD SNAKED WITH SHARP CURVES more appropriate to a mountain pass than this flat stretch of North Georgia houses and small farm plots. But it was the boy's road. Kyle Edwards rode his bicycle on it daily. It was only about two miles long. On one end was the Sweetwater Reservoir where Kyle bought fifteen-cent candy at the dank bait shop that smelled of earthworms, crickets, and minnows; the other end intersected Lee Road, the two-lane blacktop.

It was a safe world—more or less. There were only three things in Kyle's world that he considered dangerous and that he feared. One was the territorial bull that roamed the cow pasture that bordered the cornfield. The pasture held the green pond where Kyle liked to spend a great deal of his time, so whenever he went there, he had to be vigilant of the bull that had already crippled one boy from the area.

His other fear was of Patrick Sewell and his little brother Joel and their friend Scotty Clonts. They were teenagers. Long hair and dirty Levis. Scotty Clonts seemed to wear the same shirt every day—a T-shirt with cut-off sleeves that had the words *Judas Priest—Sad Wings of Destiny* printed on it in gothic script. Kyle didn't know what a Judas Priest was, but it struck him as menacing—as did Scotty himself. Patrick Sewell was the oldest son of Nathan Sewell, the chairman of the Douglas County Board of Commissioners. Nathan Sewell somehow managed to get himself reelected every four years despite the fact that his son Patrick was an unemployed high school dropout (hell, they kicked him out, most folks would say) who sported frizzy red hippie hair, seldom bathed, and was suspected to be involved with drugs.

Patrick had once thrown a brick at Kyle, unprovoked, while he was riding his bike. The brick had hit him in the chest and knocked him off his bicycle into a ditch. The blow had knocked the breath out of Kyle's lungs, and he had lain in the ditch, momentarily unable to breathe and certain he was going to die, Patrick standing over him, laughing.

Patrick's younger brother, Joel, was the same age as Kyle, but he was scared of Joel most of all. Joel was disfigured. The lower half of his face was a twisted raw mess. Kyle's oldest brother, Jason, said that Joel Sewell had drunk a bottle of Drano, and the acid had eaten away his lower jaw and throat. Supposedly, Joel thought it was Coca-Cola he was drinking, but that didn't make any sense to Kyle. How could you confuse Drano with Coca-Cola?

Kyle rode his bike (a hand-me-down Schwinn Stingray complete with gold glitter banana seat and ape hanger handlebars) as fast and as hard as he could up and down Eden Road, delighting in the plumes of red dust he kicked up behind him. He rode straight down the center, never giving the remotest thought to his safety. He was just a boy.

He was scared of only one other thing in his environment—and that was blasting caps. Public safety commercials about blasting caps seemed to interrupt every cartoon he ever watched, typically depicting a boy about Kyle's age, walking through dirt and debris—as he himself often did—and spying a benign and compact bundle of wires half obscured on the ground. The boy in the commercial always did exactly what Kyle would have done lucking up on such a fascinating treasure: He picked it up and began fidgeting with it. The commercial ended with a look of surprised horror in the commercial boy's eyes, the screen going to white, and the echoing thunder of an explosion fading out.

The commercials worked on Kyle's mother as well, creeping into her mind, so that she regularly admonished him that if he ever came across anything that looked like a blasting cap, he should not touch it, but come straight home and tell her.

So Kyle was haunted by the remote chance of being blown to bits, but he exercised zero caution playing in the road. No one had ever warned him. Certainly not his parents. There'd been no commercials.

HE WAS PEDALING THE BIKE STANDING UP, going for maximum speed, maximum dust trails, heading straight into a blind curve, when the blue car materialized in front of him. There was time for him to note that the car was kicking up its own massive trail of dust, denoting high speed. There was also time for Kyle to note that he was dead. Even in his limited understanding of the world, he could see that the coming collision was neither avoidable nor survivable. The car was going to hit him— that seemed a given. And it would kill him. Another given. At ten years old, he understood that tons of hurtling metal versus a boy on a bicycle equaled death.

He watched, as though a bystander, the scene of his own demise.

The last thing he saw before he hit the dirt was the woman behind the wheel of the powder blue Chevelle Super Sport, her face dumb, not yet comprehending. Kyle laid down his bike, skidding toward the car's bumper. And the woman must have done something, because when Kyle finally opened his eyes, he was completely unharmed. Fresh skid marks ended two feet away from where he sat in the road. He inspected his body, making sure that it was true, that he was unhurt; then he picked up his bike, which was a little dusty but also unharmed. When he tried to mount the bicycle, he fell over it, his legs refusing to work properly. When he was able to get back up, he started pushing his bicycle back toward his driveway.

Up ahead, he saw the Chevelle SS, resting on its side, the undercarriage exposed, the top two wheels spinning. He heard glass breaking and cascading down the side of the car. The woman had somehow popped out the passenger side window (which would have been above her head from inside the car). Kyle watched her mount the steering column and crawl out of the window, emerging bloody and disheveled like a violent birth. She slid down over the hood and dropped to her feet. They stood facing each other, neither of them able to move. The woman broke her inertia and lurched toward Kyle. Kyle took a step forward.

The driveway leading back to the safety of Kyle's home lay between him and the woman. She was much closer to it than Kyle, but she was moving slow, stumbling, dazed. Their eyes were locked as they moved toward each other.

"Help me turn my car over. Help me turn my car over. Help me turn my car over."

She said it like a record stuck in a groove. No emotion, just quiet, flawed logic. But Kyle knew there was no way that even together they could budge the automobile. A grown man might could rock it back over to its wheels, but not a boy and an injured woman. And even if they could, this bleeding shambling woman was not going to be able to get in and drive away as if nothing had happened. He instinctively knew that more than just her body had been damaged, that something was wrong with her mind.

He beat her to the driveway and started walking down it backward, rolling his bicycle and keeping the reticulated woman in his vision. He did not know what she was going to do, but she was still asking him to help her turn over the car. And Kyle wished he could. He wished that they could flip it back onto its wheels and the bleeding woman could just drive away and that this truly terrible thing had not ever happened.

THE GRAVEL DRIVEWAY FROM THE ROAD to the house was a good eighth of a mile long. Houses in this pocket of the barely rural South were built with little concern of land usage, because land was plentiful and mostly cheap. The Edwards house was built amongst a dying breed—the local small farmer. Instead of a yard, the house had actively growing fields all around it. Facing the house, on the left side of the driveway, was dense corn that held the driveway like a painted green retaining wall, and to the right was a field of low-growing sweet potatoes edged with sickly looking peanut plants. In the late summer, Daddy-Bob, the farmer who owned most all the land on Eden Road, would pay Kyle and his brothers a quarter per bushel basket to harvest the peanuts, and the same again in the fall to harvest the sweet potatoes. Often, his mama and daddy would join in the work as well, and Kyle liked it when they did. There was just something that satisfied him when the whole family worked as a single unit. It was at those times that they seemed closest. And he somehow understood that his parents joined in not for the money, but because they too enjoyed the work.

This was food planted not in quantities to fill cargo trucks and be shipped to grocery stores, but for Daddy-Bob's produce stand that stood at the top of the dirt road—with the excess going to the local farmer's market.

Kyle much preferred working the potatoes and peanuts to picking the corn. The corn was planted in staggered fashion, and started coming in during midsummer when it was still hot as fire, the air wet and adhesive like syrup. The thick frond-like leaves of the corn plants would roughly grab hold of Kyle's exposed skin, rubbing it raw, sometimes cutting. And the plants seemed to hold on to their treasured ears of corn, giving them up only grudgingly, making him fight for each one, so that he was covered in sweat and sap, forearms already raw, before he could fill even a single bushel. And the corn seemed to emit a kind of sticky secretion that slowly covered you and attracted dirt and insects. It was hard, sweaty, sometimes ugly work.

But the sweet potatoes and the peanuts were a joy. It was usually cooler when they were ready to be harvested. And the fashion of the harvesting was a constant delight to Kyle's senses. He was given a pitchfork that was easily a foot longer than he was. The tines of the instrument were wickedly long, clotted with red dirt and orange rust from the long years of their useful life. The wood handles were blanched gray from weathering, and worn smooth as river stone from generations of workers' hands. The handles were also worn skinny about six inches from the top where a callused hand would naturally hold it during work.

Just like Daddy-Bob had taught him, Kyle would pick a spot

about a foot-and-a-half beyond the farthest reach of the plant's leaves. The fork had to be angled so that once it penetrated the earth, the tines would extend under the plant, about center. Kyle, who was small for his age, and pale even in summertime, would stand up on the pitchfork, both feet resting atop, behind the tines, and once stable, he would grab hold of the handle and jump up, both feet coming back down squarely, setting the tines in the earth. It took three or four good jumps. And once the fork was buried, Kyle would throw his entire body weight against the handle, to loosen the sun-hardened earth. Then he would get behind and pull back on the pitchfork.

At that time of year, the outer showing of the potato plant was puny, even dead looking, so it was always a wonder for Kyle to watch the fork lift the plant out of the ground from the bottom up, and see the unimaginable profundity of sweet potatoes cradled in the fork. The dirt would fall away through the wide tines, leaving the fat bulbous potatoes resting pretty. A single plant could sometimes fill half a bushel basket. Some of the potatoes would be as big and long as a loaf of bread, some as small as marbles. At first, Kyle would often drive a tine of the pitchfork through a potato, splitting it or scarring it, but soon he developed a sense for how they lay and never even nicked one.

The peanuts were harvested the same way, with the pitchfork lifting them from the earth, hard shells clotted with dirt, later to be washed and sold boiled at Daddy-Bob's stand.

SHE WAS STILL COMING AT HIM, ARMS OUT-
stretched, her pace as slow as Boris Karloff. In his line of sight, as
though staged for a photograph that would capture the essential
details of the scene, Kyle could see the woman's blue car, on its
side in the ditch, the wheels no longer spinning, the windshield
white and opaque like a caterpillar's cocoon, and as still as death.
It was with the potatoes and peanuts to his right, and the vastness
of the corn to his left, that Kyle finally found the courage to hop
on his bicycle and turn his back on the broken woman.

His bike kicked up a modest dust trail (white, from the crushed
gravel surface) as he pedaled at high speed back to his house. He
propped his bike against the brick wall in the shadowy carport,
and walked into the house. The door from the carport opened into
the laundry room, and both the washer and dryer were humming
and the good scents of detergent and fabric softener hung hu-
midly in the air. The laundry room led directly into the kitchen,
and in the kitchen Kyle found his mother standing over the coun-

ter making pineapple sandwiches. His little sister, Grace, sat at the redwood picnic bench that served as the family's dining table. Grace held her Wonder Woman doll in one hand and sucked the thumb of the other while she watched their mother work.

"Hungry?" his mother asked.

Kyle watched her slather mayonnaise over a row of Sunbeam bread slices laid out on the counter like a hand of solitaire. She dipped a single extended finger into an open can of cored pineapple, bringing out the entire contents, her index finger and knuckles supporting the pineapple slices at their hollow core. She shook off the juice and placed a round wedge on each piece of bread.

Kyle nodded and sat down across from his sister at the picnic table.

"You okay?"

Kyle looked away from his mother and said, "It's hot is all."

His mother nodded, told Grace to stop sucking her thumb before it fell off, and reached to one of the high cabinets and brought down a can of Charles Chips. They were potato chips that were delivered twice a month. They came in a tin the size of a hatbox, and the Charles Chips deliveryman would always stop and talk to Kyle in a way that made Kyle feel good.

Right now Kyle just didn't know what to do or say. How could he tell his mother what had happened? It had been his fault. The whole thing had been his fault. He'd been riding in the middle of the road, on a blind curve. And now a broken bleeding woman was on her way to the front door, to lay the blame squarely at Kyle's feet. Kyle couldn't imagine what words existed to be able to tell his mother this. This was the most real thing that had ever happened to him.

He had heard of awful things happening in this world, but they did not happen in his little part of the world. And he certainly had never been the cause of a Bad Thing. One Bad Thing that happened in the world was caught in his mind as a constant reminder of just how bad the world could actually be. He had been riding in the car with his father, and the news was on the radio, and the newsman was talking about people being beat up for their money in a laundrymat. And that one of the bad guys had taken a ballpoint pen and punctured the eardrum of one of the people. And Kyle had never realized until that time that truly horrible things could happen to a person. Having a ballpoint pen driven into your ear and puncturing something inside you was a violation he had never imagined possible. Or that one person would do something like that to another person. Why?

He was familiar with laundrymats. Before his family had their own washer and dryer, his mother used to take him and Grace to a coin-operated laundrymat once a week. It had always seemed like a safe place to Kyle, warm with good smells and lots of women. But now, he realized that if that thing with the ballpoint pen had happened in a laundrymat, then that thing could have potentially happened to him. Truly horrible, violent things could happen to him.

And now it had. And he was the one who had caused it.

He ate his pineapple sandwich, surprised that it still tasted good and that he still had an appetite. The glass of milk was cold and it tasted good too. He even asked for more Charles Chips, but his mother said no because they were so expensive. He had decided that since he did not have the words to tell his mother what had happened, he would just let it happen. That was the best way.

The woman should be here any second, scratching at the door with her nailless fingers, the dried spiderweb of blood on her face branding her. So he finished his lunch and went to the living room and waited.

But the woman never came. Kyle spent the rest of the day in the bedroom playing Operation with Grace, and that night the whole family watched *Hee Haw* (which he really didn't like) and then *The Brady Bunch* on TV. He loved to sing along to the Brady Bunch theme song, and he did so that night. He had learned that it was possible to be scared and carry a burden of fear and worry and guilt, and still behave normally.

His daddy never did say anything, and he would have driven right past the wreck on his way home after his Saturday shift at the mail sorting plant.

What had happened to the woman?

BEFORE CHURCH THE NEXT DAY, AND BEING careful not to dirty his Sunday clothes, Kyle took his bicycle out to the end of the driveway, stopped, and peered up and down the dirt road. There was no evidence of what had happened yesterday. It was like it had not happened at all. Kyle did not understand how this was possible, but he was just a boy. And while he did realize that probably God had intervened to save him, he gave no more thought to what had happened until the police lady came to the door later that day.

WITH THE PERSPECTIVE OF ADULTHOOD, the man who the boy became would realize that there was a dividing line in his life, a border that, once crossed, would tinge everything that happened after, and dim all events prior. That border was a swatch of time, the space of a single summer. He was ten years old, and his sister, his partner in that strange borderland, was three years younger. The year was 1976.

It was a dividing time for America as well. The year Kyle Edwards turned ten, America celebrated its two-hundredth birthday, and everything that happened that year was somehow informed by the genocide, the slavery, the savage wars, and the casual cruelties that had gotten them, as a nation, to that point in time.

Of course, Kyle was mostly unaware of any of this. He was not precocious or insightful or strikingly bright. He was just a boy.

He was only aware that it was a special year, that during that year, everybody was a patriot. As far as the world at large went, Kyle had accumulated only a handful of basic facts: He knew that the news stories about Watergate that his daddy took such interest in had finally sputtered to an end (although he still did not understand what a Watergate was), Patty Hearst had been found guilty (of what he didn't know), and Vietnam was finally really over. The searing image of a naked Vietnamese girl running from a black bloom of napalm was replaced in his mind by the ubiquitous "Bicentennial Minute"—those patriotic commercials that came on every night right before nine o'clock, Kyle's bedtime.

That year, everybody felt good about America.

But in the summer of 1976, Kyle Edwards was ten years old, and his world was an insular one. His world was a red dirt road in rural Georgia. A rural Georgia that was fast becoming suburban. County workers would lay down asphalt on Eden Road before the year was over, and backhoes and graders would break the earth all along it to build massive subdivisions.

In Kyle's world, his family's personal Vietnam was only just beginning. His parents, the warring factions, were in an arms race, each side amassing weapons for the divorce that was to come. And like Americans who watched the bloody conflict unfold on their television screens, Kyle and his sister Grace, and their two older brothers, Jason and Wade, watched the war develop. A cold war, really. Resentments and suspicions building beneath the surface. They were fascinated and horrified, unable to look away, unable to alter its course.

The oldest brother, Jason, was six years older than Kyle, so he would have been sixteen that year. Wade was next at thirteen, then Kyle, and Grace was seven. They were all three years apart. Kyle was supposed to have been a girl. Their mother had already bore two sons and very much wanted a baby girl, but got Kyle instead. She tried a final time and succeeded with Grace.

AND ACROSS THE ROAD, WATCHING THEM
that summer from his wheeled metal perch, was the paralyzed
man. He grew into a mythical figure that haunted Kyle. He had
been there on Eden Road for Kyle's entire life, and before he became the paralyzed man, he was just a cipher to Kyle, just "that
man who lives across the road," or "that man from church who
passes the collection plate." He was aware of him, but he was no
more important to Kyle than a pine tree, a vague point of reference in his world. Then just a few days after Kyle caused the
woman to wreck her car, Mama said Mr. Ahearn from across the
road had a stroke and that they had to put him in the hospital.
And then the workmen had been at his house a week or so later,
building a ramp that sloped down from his front porch. When Mr.
Ahearn got back from the hospital, Kyle's mother took over some
peach preserves with the special yellow ribbon tied around it. His
mama had said to his daddy that Mr. Ahearn was paralyzed. She
whispered the word when she said it. And then Kyle started to see

him sitting out there on his porch, day after day, just sitting there, sunning himself like a salamander. Day after day sitting in that big metal chair with wheels on it.

To kyle and grace, he became less a point of reference, and more a landmark. He was The Paralyzed Man, and they shunned him.

GRACE AND KYLE WERE PLAYING HIDE-
and-seek in the cornfield that bordered their property and
stretched up to Eden Road. The corn was getting full and heavy
with fat ears. Floppy golden tassels of corn silk cascaded from the
crowns. The leaves were thick, abrasive, and sharp. They poked
out from the stalks at odd angles and would cut them quick if they
weren't careful. Already, the field smelled of humid decay. And entering the dense rows was like stepping into an alien world. Inside, it was dark, dense, and tight when only moments before they
had been in the open, in the sunshine.

Grace carried her little plastic Wonder Woman doll with her
at all times. No exceptions. And so Wonder Woman accompanied
them as well. Kyle didn't think Grace trusted him to protect her,
but she trusted Wonder Woman. The cornfield could be a scary
place. When you're seven like Grace was that year, the whole world
can be a scary place.

* * *

I**T'S RIDICULOUSLY EASY TO HIDE IN A**
cornfield. And just as easy to get lost. It's impossible to see from
one row of corn to the next. Like a maze with but a single re-
peated turn, but still deceptively complex. Hide-and-seek in those
circumstances was less about finding someone with your eyes, but
more with your other senses. And Kyle cheated. Whenever Kyle
heard Grace getting close, he would position himself a few yards
up from her, listen to time it just right, and then step backward
out of the row just as she stepped into it—so that he ended up
behind her. At that point, he would invert the game and begin to
follow her. He would track silently behind her, match her step for
step, and smirk at her growing frustration. At times he could literally be inches away from her, hidden in a row that she'd already
searched and wouldn't think of searching again. He'd watch, delighted, as her frustration escalated to agitation, which eventually
gave way to fear. Then panic.

She would shout his name, "Kyle! Kyle!"

But he wouldn't respond. He knew Grace would be thinking
about Soap Sally, the brain-damaged boogeywoman Mama told
them about to get them to be good. *You better stop it, or Soap Sally'll
come get you tonight.* Soap Sally had needle-fingers that she stabbed
little kids with.

"Kyyyyyyyle!"

Kyle would throw a dirt clod over to the left to distract and
frighten her.

"Please, Kyyyyyyyyyyyle!"

He would time it so that he would reveal himself only at the last possible moment, only when he was certain her little mind couldn't take another second of the fear, that she would crumple and her brain would just split, irrevocably scarring her. And then he would reach out from right behind her, touching the back of her neck, fingers slithering like a snake. Or poking like needles.

And he'd revel in the scream.

Years later, when Kyle thought back on these times, he would think, *Jesus, I was a bastard.*

HE WOULD RATHER HAVE BEEN PLAYING with Jason and Wade, but his older brothers had their own worlds to explore and didn't want Kyle tagging along. It was Wade and Jason. And Kyle and Grace. Simple as that.

There were three bedrooms in their brick ranch-style house—one for their parents, one for Grace, and one for the three boys. Kyle slept with Jason in Jason's bed. And at some point, as Jason entered his teenage years, Jason bribed Kyle with a nightly nickel to go sleep in Grace's bed. Looking back, Kyle could hardly blame him—he was a teenager after all. And, frankly, Kyle wet the bed more nights than not. He supposed few boys of Jason's age would care too much to wake up in a pool of someone else's urine. Wade wet the bed too. More so than Kyle. For them to share a bed would have been a disaster. Pee would have cascaded over the rubber mattress cover and warped the wood floor beneath.

But Kyle gladly took Jason's nickel. His bed was a twin, and the two of them just barely fit in it. And Jason's growing body pushed Kyle's small frame to the floor many nights. Grace slept in a full-size bed. Why their parents never noticed the discrepancy of a teenager and a ten-year-old sharing the narrow rectangle of a twin bed versus putting a seven-year-old in the vast expanse of a full-size was just one of those family mysteries that would never be addressed to anybody's satisfaction.

THE SLEEPING ARRANGEMENT WAS THE beginning of the pattern that was set for their sibling relationships. Wade and Jason simply did not want their little brother to enter their secret existence.

Tree houses were built and camouflaged high in treetops—elaborate constructions with trapdoors and drop-down ladders made of knotted rope that could be pulled high and away from Kyle's outstretched hands. And should those outstretched hands linger too long, the tree house was stocked with weapons of Jason's creation—slingshot rifles powered by the industrial six-foot-long rubber bands their father brought home from his job as a mail handler. The rubber bands were used to secure mail pallets. They were incredibly strong and seemingly had no breaking point no matter how far they were stretched. The rubber band could power a slingshot rifle (constructed from just the right tree branch) with such force that an acorn shot from one could easily bring down a bird, or shatter a squirrel's skull. Or leave a welt on Kyle's back for three days.

Jason also constructed a gun—a real gun—from a bicycle spoke. He took a spoke, unscrewed the tiny metal cap at one end and packed match-head shavings (or black powder from a fire-cracker) into the little hollow cavity of the metal cap. He would then screw the cap back in reverse so that the hollow end was now pointing out. Then he would bend the opposite end of the spoke into a grip handle like a revolver. Last, Jason would find a BB pellet or tiny rock and jam it down into the hollow powder-packed cavity. Once prepared, the cap end was held over a candle flame or a lit match until the powder ignited and shot the tiny rock with enough force to pierce flesh.

Kyle spied from afar. Later that summer he followed them over a two-mile trek through the woods behind their house to the sandy banks of Sweetwater Creek. The trip to get there had been a long and scary one for Kyle. He had never ventured that far on foot in his entire life. It was a fine line of keeping up with them and, at the same time, not being caught following them. Luckily, Kyle's systematic terrorization of Grace in the cornfields had honed his abilities of tracking and concealment to a razor sharp degree.

He stayed behind and watched from the edge of the woods as they entered an open, sunny space. The pine needle surface gave way not to the hard packed red dirt and clay Kyle was used to see-ing, but rather the ground swelled up to a sandy, loamy bank. Jason and Wade crested the embankment and disappeared, down, out of

Kyle's sight. He waited a minute, knowing that the open space would make him a target easily spotted—and leaving himself open to God knows what type of devious and elaborate punishment Jason might construct with no parents within earshot to rein him in.

JASON WAS SMART. HE WAS THE MASTER-
mind behind the forts, the tunnels, the handmade weapons. And
often those weapons were used as punishment against his little
brother for following him and Wade. Jason—and it was always
Jason—came up with elaborate, sometimes Goldbergian, punish-
ments. Wade was his drone, not the instigator. Jason was brilliant
in a Fu Manchu manner.

Once, Jason and Wade took Kyle out into the cow pasture that
lay just beyond the cornfields. It was a good ways out. First
through the cornfield that abutted their driveway, then under the
tangled barbed wire fence that enclosed the cow pasture. They
headed for a shade tree oasis on the far side of the pasture. Kyle
noted that both Jason and Wade would steal quick glances over
their shoulders, as though they thought they were being followed.
Then he realized that they were just watching out for Buddy the
bull.

Buddy was a massive Holstein, old and grizzled with yellowed horns, and known far and wide for his ill temper. At least two thousand pounds, Buddy would charge any interlopers in his pasture. But he was old and spent most days dozing on his feet. One only had to be vigilant and very quiet to ensure safe passage.

The summer before, a group of local teens made a Saturday afternoon sport of it, a weekly poor-man's running of the bulls. It was Patrick Sewell (being the county chairman's son, Patrick felt he could do anything he damn well pleased—and he was mostly right), Patrick's younger brother, the facially disfigured Joel, and Patrick's two disciples: Scotty Clonts and Darl Graybeal. They would gather in the middle of the pasture and drink beer—growing progressively louder until Buddy took notice. From that point it became a game of chicken. The cluster of teens would watch as Buddy first took notice, then worked his way slyly toward them. Buddy would munch at the grass or move along the barbed wire fence as though something on the other side had caught his attention—all the while making his way almost imperceptibly toward the interlopers.

But they knew what Buddy was working up to, and they would giggle nervously and finish up their beers. The bull's movements would grow steadily more intent, more obvious. The shambling steps became a trot, then a gallop, then a full-blown charge. And the teens would huddle even tighter, eyeing each other to see who was chicken, who would be the first to break ranks. Once the circle was broken, once the survival instincts of one sane member of the group finally overrode social conformity, the group would scatter like a perfect break shot in a game of pool.

From the scattering, the massive bull would pick his victim—

maybe he chose by vicinity, or maybe some primitive instinct allowed the bull to instantly identify the weakest one. Buddy was old, a hulking, lumbering, gnarled nightmare. And the teens always managed to hop or scuttle under the rusty barbed wire fence well ahead of him. Until the day Darl Graybeal stepped in a gopher hole. If Darl hadn't been the one that Buddy had chosen to pursue, it wouldn't have mattered. He could have crawled under the fence to safety while Buddy charged one of the others. But Darl was the one Buddy had singled out.

He'd been teasing the bull, playing cat-and-mouse around the trunk of a massive oak. Darl had just made his break from the tree, and was dashing wildly but confidently for the fence. The others were cheering him on from their safe havens on the other side of the barbed wire. The boy reveled in the attention. But then his foot came down in the hole, and the cheering stopped. The snapping sound as Darl's ankle broke was loud enough for everyone to hear. As was the scream that directly followed.

The others later agreed that what came next seemed to occur in slow motion. The boy made it back up to his knees, and—everyone also agreed—if he'd just simply rolled to one side or the other, he'd have been okay, it would have bought him time to evade the bull, to at least get back to the relative safety of the oak tree. But that's not what Darl did. He tried to stand and the pain from his ankle caused him to immediately sink back down to his knees. Two thousand pounds of Buddy the Bull caught him square in the back. The horns didn't gore him, they didn't pierce his skin, but the force of the blow broke his spinal column. The crack was far louder than the ankle break had been. Darl didn't get back up or move at all. (He in fact never moved again—except for being able to blink his eyes, an ability that he used for the rest of his life to communicate in Morse code.)

The lack of movement probably saved his life. While the boy lay motionless, Buddy sniffed him. Darl, conscious through it all, could feel warm, slimy stringers of slobber and mucus from the bull's mouth and nose grease his bare arms and neck. Patrick, Joel, and Scotty watched, not believing this had happened to one of their own. But it had. And after a few more nudges, the bull was satisfied that this particular interloper would move no more (and he was right). Buddy finally headed off for the green pond to quench his thirst after this hot work, but first he seemed to gaze at the shocked teenagers, a sullen, proud look to his dark eyes, as though daring them to try him again.

The teens waited a solid thirty minutes before entering the pasture and retrieving their fallen friend. They lifted his broken body over the fence, and laid him in the vinyl backseat of Patrick's Chevy Malibu. Three times on the way to the hospital, they had to pull over and reposition Darl because the boy's limp, yielding body slid off the seat at every turn. After the fourth time, they just left his crumpled form on the floorboard, and by the time they got to the hospital, they'd agreed upon a story that centered around the three of them trying to talk Darl out of his foolhardy intention of testing the bull, but Darl just wouldn't listen to reason, and they suspected he might have been drinking beer before they met up with him. Scotty Clonts threw in that last bit about the beer, and they all nodded in unison at the perfection of the story. Darl listened to them from the floorboard, and he knew that in their position, he would have done the same.

Darl graybeal's shattered spinal column was very much on Kyle's mind on the day of "the experiment." Jason and Wade took Kyle as far as the stagnant green pond that was concealed under a ring of towering weeping willow trees. The trees were massive with long thick cascading curtains of greenery. They gave dense shade. The green pond itself was dark and clotted with algae. Like a noxious soup, the green flotsam simmered as it gave off fetid bubbles of oxygen, the bubbles often trapped under the thick layer of scum that floated on top. It was where the cows drank.

Kyle was delighted to be included in whatever grand adventure his brothers might have in mind. Once at the green pond, Jason sat him down at the trunk of a willow tree and explained that they wanted to perform an experiment. He thus produced two rough strands of hemp rope. He lashed Kyle's legs together at the ankles. Kyle didn't protest. Again, he was just so very happy to be a part of their adventure. He would go along with anything to be included. The second piece of rope secured his hands behind his back. The hemp fibers were scratchy and bit into his wrists.

"Okay. We're gonna do a little experiment. You want to?"

Kyle nodded his head.

"Let's see if you can make it back home before Buddy gets you."

Kyle nodded again. This was crazy, but not overly so. The key was discretion. Kyle looked over his shoulder and saw Buddy dozing in a far corner under the shade of a mimosa bough. They had yet to draw his attention, and even if they had, Buddy was wont to sidle up to his targets, taking his time and edging closer, ever closer before striking. Kyle was safe unless he did something foolish.

Jason gave him a curt nod, and Wade pulled a single Black Cat firecracker and a kitchen match out of his jeans pocket. They must have been saving the firecracker for a long time. It looked pretty beat-up, its gray fuse kinked and frayed. Wade struck the match on a rock. In a single fluid motion, he lit the fuse and tossed the firecracker.

Jason and Wade were off, running at full speed before the Black Cat landed. In the open field, the report was like a rifle shot, seeming to echo even though there were no barriers to bounce sound. Kyle looked across the pasture and saw the bull was looking directly at him. He let out a single, aggressive bellow. Then Buddy's bowels let loose, and a river of fecal matter pooled into a brown patty the consistency of loose oatmeal at his rear hoofs. Kyle was too far away to hear the splatting sound.

Buddy was an intact bull, and even at this distance, Kyle could see the pendulum of his considerable reproductive apparatus swing heavily beneath him as he lumbered into motion.

Kyle could play dead, he had done that before, and it always worked, but instinctively he knew that this time it wouldn't. The firecracker had been too loud, too threatening. And Buddy had already marked him. And he was not wasting time with his sly sidling routine. Buddy was not attempting to camouflage his intentions; he was heading straight for Kyle.

Kyle still had time. Buddy was old. It took him a while to get his considerable mass moving at speed. Kyle leapt to his feet and hopped. With his hands and feet tied, hopping was all that he could do. Kyle hopped toward the fence, amazed at the progress adrenaline was helping him to make, but Buddy was building up speed. Good speed. Looking over his shoulder, Kyle saw him taking great, earthshaking bounds, slavering and snorting in rage. He judged the distance to the fence versus Buddy's looming progress, and realized that it was just not possible to get out of this without severe injury. He was going to be gored and possibly trampled.

He hopped faster—looked like a boy on an invisible pogo stick—but still he knew it was useless. It was a race hopelessly lost.

"Kyyyyyle!"

It was Grace, but in his mad hopping dash, he couldn't spot her. "Kyyyyyyle!"

And then he caught the glint of shining metal off to one side. It was Wonder Woman's bullet-deflecting bracelets. Grace was waving Wonder Woman over her head and calling his name to get his attention.

To his left, the pasture sloped sharply downward to the woods. At the bottom of the slope, there was Grace, behind the fence.

She was now bent over, pulling on the lowest strand of the barbed wire, lifting it to give Kyle easy passage. Daddy-Bob had strung the fence with five levels of wire, the first level only six inches off the ground, so that it was almost impossible to get under the fence without someone there to lift the bottom strand.

Kyle could now feel the vibrations of Buddy's hoofs shaking the ground. He kept hopping, knowing it was useless, that he could not win, but that he must make a choice. The fence line straight ahead of Kyle that bordered the cornfield was at least fifty yards closer than the line to his left, and their innumerable forays into the pasture had created a divot at that spot where it was possible to get under the fence alone, but even then, it was a slow, painstaking process to carefully wriggle under it without being cut on the rusty barbs.

"Kyyyyyyle!"

He hopped like a startled rabbit, able to feel the ground vibrate from Buddy's presence even while in midjump. A mad bellow exploded in his ears, and Kyle felt hot breath and slobber on his neck.

Kyle broke to his left. Buddy was not able to turn his freight train of speeding bulk in kind, but he made a deft curve and would easily intersect with Kyle ten yards from the fence—there was just no way Kyle could move any faster. It was over. There was nowhere to hide. Kyle was caught.

And then it came to him. Instead of struggling to keep his balance on the steep hill, Kyle dropped to his side and rolled. The rope binding his limbs worked to his advantage. It held his body in a tight cylinder as Kyle rolled with amazing, scary speed to the bottom of the hill. Each revolution of his body allowed him a stop-motion snapshot of Grace at the bottom. He saw her using every shred of her strength to lift the taut bottom wire high enough and wide enough to give him safe passage—but never letting go of Wonder Woman. For the rest of his life, Kyle would be able to clearly recall her beautiful little girl's face grimaced with exertion. Why had he been such a shit to her? She was his best friend. She was good and true.

And Kyle rolled deftly under the fence, not even nicked by the sharp barbs of steel. Rolling, Kyle took Grace's legs out from under her like a bowling pin, and she landed on top of him, laughing. They laughed together, Kyle almost hysterical, with Wonder Woman pinned between them.

After that, Grace was his Wonder Woman. She was his best friend. It was going to be him and her. They would have their own coteries. Their own adventures. Their own secrets.

They watched Buddy trample his way toward them, unable to alter his homicidal charge, and for a moment Grace and Kyle thought it had all been pyrrhic effort, as Buddy was surely going to come right through the fence and trample them both. But he was able to divert himself before hitting the fence with full force; in his turn he brushed the fence, causing it to bow out under his weight. And he bellowed in frustration and pain as the barbs caught his flesh, rending it in three long ragged streaks.

Daddy-Bob knew the value of a dollar, and no part of an animal ever went to waste. Years later, after Buddy had died of simple old age, a young married couple from Atlanta looking to furnish their first home would be standing in a Havertys furniture showroom listening intently as a salesman extolled the beauty of a sectional leather couch. The salesman would point out the fine grain of the leather as he ran his fingers along a triptych of imperfections and say that this natural scarring from the animal's life gave the leather character.

Aᴎᴅ ꜱᴏ ᴋʏʟᴇ ᴛʀᴀᴄᴋᴇᴅ ʜɪꜱ ʙʀᴏᴛʜᴇʀꜱ ᴛᴏ the creek's banks—where they had descended and disappeared from his line of sight. From the woods, he watched the creek bank for any further signs of them. He was about to approach, but found himself still cautious, hesitant. He sensed that they were still close by, perhaps lying in wait for him. Perhaps devising another experiment.

A wisp of smoke rose and curled above the red clay bank. It carried to him and he could smell the acidic, sharp smell of burning pine. They had built a campfire. Kyle imagined they must be camping out at the water's edge, maybe even fishing for crawfish to boil or a catfish to fry. Jealousy stung him hard. This was what Kyle wanted. Building fires and pretending to live in the woods. These were the adventures he wanted—not being relegated to piddling games of treasure hunt and hide-and-seek with a seven-year-old girl. Thus, in that wisp of campfire smoke, did his recent fealty to Grace dissipate.

Kyle ducked behind a pine branch when he caught sight of his brothers cresting the creek bank. Jason said, "I saw some good ones about half a mile down from here," and they took off running.

Once he was certain that they were gone, Kyle crossed over and descended the bank. The creek water looked rusty, its flow sluggish. He could find no sign of a fire, no evidence that Jason and Wade had been here at all. He looked up and down the creek, but there was nothing. Kyle started climbing back up the bank when he saw it. Just a bit to the left, a hole, an *excavation*, in the middle of the earthen bank. It was the opening to a cave. A tendril of smoke licked the top and drifted out.

He studied it from the outside before going inside. There was a stone-encircled fire pit in the middle, and candles burning here and there placed in hollowed-out little cubbies and rock shelves. Even with the flames, it was dark inside, but Kyle could see a pickax and a shovel. He knew that his brothers must have dug this cave in the bank themselves. There was no evidence of it outside the cave, so they must have scattered the excavations into the creek to hide all evidence.

Kyle stepped inside, and he could feel the weight of the damp sand and clay pushing down on him, wanting to collapse. At the rear of the cave, the wall gave way to two tunnels that were dark as midnight. He wanted out of there. Even his ten-year-old mind knew that this was a death trap. A cave-in waiting to happen. But he was struck by the fact that the cave was, more than anything else, a virtual armory. Everywhere he looked were knife-sharpened spears made from tree limbs, bloodweed javelins, spoke guns, slingshot rifles, elderberry blowguns, clothespin match throwers, and more. It was like Jason and Wade were preparing for war.

And they must have been preparing for a very long time. The bloodweed javelins had to be harvested in the fall when the stalks died and hardened—making a six-foot-long spear that whistled through the air with a brutally sharp taproot that could easily pierce skin. There must have been more than a hundred of them. Kyle picked one up and let his finger play over the sharp tip. The end where the taproot had been cut still oozed blood-colored sap. He put it back and was ready to get out of there when he felt vibrations in the clay. Footsteps. Someone was approaching. Kyle heard voices directly above him. He recognized the voice of Patrick Sewell.

"Man, that boy's car still smells like bad pussy."

"I'd rather have bad pussy than no pussy." Must have been Scotty Clonts.

"How would you know, queer boy? You ain't never touched any kind of pussy."

"More than you."

"Right, whatever you say, Clonts."

"Kiss my ass, Sewell."

Then there was a grunting sound and the thud of Scotty Clonts hitting the ground.

"Let's go man. We got work to do. Money to make."

Kyle heard them moving on, and after a minute, he climbed out of the cave and back to the top of the bank and saw Patrick, Scotty, and Joel entering the woods. He decided to follow them. Kyle had successfully tracked Jason and Wade without being detected, so he felt reasonably confident that he could now rise to the challenge of tracking more dangerous game.

He FOLLOWED THEM TO A SMALL CLEAR-
ing deeper in the woods. Kyle recognized the layout of a rectangular, cultivated patch, but the plants growing there were beyond
his scope of experience. They towered six or seven feet on thick
stalks that sprouted clumpy buds and five-leaf clusters. Patrick
had a machete, and he was slashing the most mature plants at
the base. Patrick tossed the plants to Joel or Scotty—whoever was
standing closer—and they would fasten the plants to a rope that
was strung between two pines. They hung the plants upside
down, and Kyle had seen a similar processing of plants in a to-
bacco barn where the broad leaves were fastened in bunches and
hung upside down to cure.

Mostly Kyle watched Joel Sewell. He fascinated and repelled
Kyle. How could anyone ever in a million years mistake Drano
for Coca-Cola? How was that possible? The underside of Joel's
chin and down his throat was a raw bubbly mess. It must have
hurt worse than any pain Kyle could ever imagine. Seemed like it

should be healing by now, but it always looked wet and fresh. Maybe the acid was still active in the flesh.

Something was tickling his arm, and when he looked down he saw it was a little spider—a brown recluse. Paw-Paw Edwards had lost his left foot to a brown recluse bite. His foot had just rotted off a day at a time for nine weeks. Kyle jerked and slapped and twisted and went a little haywire to get it off of him. When he looked back up, the three boys were staring right at him. It seemed to Kyle like they all looked at each other for a very long time. Finally, Patrick said, "Get him."

They all broke into action simultaneously. Kyle took off like a Black Cat bottle rocket. He was running so fast that little branches and twigs drew blood on his cheeks. Kyle didn't care. As far as he was concerned, the devil and his disciples were chasing to drag him down to hell. Kyle had seen murder in Patrick's eyes.

Scotty was the shortest, with thick little stubby legs and a body like a fire hydrant. But somehow he was the fastest. When he dared to look over his shoulder, it was Scotty Kyle saw. Closing in. His sweat-damp blond hair whipping around his square head. And that Judas Priest T-shirt. *Sad Wings of Destiny*, it said. Kyle knew that if he could just get out of his line of sight, then he could probably hide, slip under some bushes, or dive into a briar bramble. But Scotty was closing in. Then Kyle remembered his brothers' cave. If he could make it back to the creek bank, Kyle might stand a chance.

He threw a zigzag into his running, not wanting his course to be obvious, but Scotty didn't zig, and when Kyle zagged back onto his original course, Scotty was a lot closer than he had been before. Kyle's legs felt heavy and numb, but he forced them to pump harder. He had to get away from Scotty. He heard a grunt behind him. And then the thumping footfalls went silent as Scotty sailed through the air in a lunging jump. If he didn't manage to grab him, then when Scotty fell to the ground, it would buy Kyle the time to disappear over the creek bank. But Scotty did grab him. His left foot was kicked back in a long stride, and Kyle felt Scotty's hand clamp down around his ankle. Both his legs went out from under him, and Scotty and Kyle tumbled to the ground in a heap. Scotty started jabbing his fist into Kyle's ribs, punching him over and over. Then he started in on his head, finally settling in on his ears, hitting them over and over, each blow sounding like a bomb exploding in Kyle's mind. He curled up into a tight ball. Fighting back would have just made it worse.

After a while, Scotty stopped. He got to his feet and stood over Kyle like a hunter would stand over fallen prey. Patrick and Joel got there. Patrick leaned over with his hands on his knees, breathing hard. His words were ragged, and Kyle could smell decay on his breath.

"Narc. Little narc. Get up." Kyle didn't move. He just lay there curled up like a roly-poly. But he didn't have a shell to protect himself like a roly-poly, and when Patrick kicked him, the steel toe of his boot landed on his spinal column, sending rolling waves of pain reverberating up and down his body. "Get up."

Kyle uncurled and sat up, looking at them to see what was next. Patrick still had his machete in his hand, and Kyle could imagine him cutting off his head and burying him out here in the woods. Or maybe they might do something crazy to him like those people in the laundrymat had busted that man's eardrum out with a ballpoint pen.

Patrick snatched Kyle up onto his feet and shook him like a dirty rug. "You a spy? You like spying on folks? Scotty, remember what they did to spies during the Rebellion?" Patrick shoved him to Scotty. Scotty was about the same height as Kyle, but he was sturdy and thick as a tree trunk, and when Kyle slammed into him, the impact was so solid he thought Patrick had shoved him into a tree.

Scotty turned Kyle to face him and said, "They used to put out their eyes. So they couldn't spy no more." With that, Scotty pushed him backward, and when he came to a stop, Kyle felt Joel Sewell's thin arms around him. Joel was actually the same age as Kyle, but in school he hung out with the older kids. Kyle remembered that before he ruined his face, Joel had just been a shy kid that kept to himself. It was only after he drank the Drano that he started hanging out with the big kids, his brother's friends. And when he thought about it as an adult, Kyle realized that the kids his own age were too scared of Joel to be his friend.

Kyle looked up right into the bubbly red scar tissue that was the underside of Joel's chin.

"Hold him right there," Patrick said, and Joel's arms slipped through Kyle's, hands clasped behind Kyle's neck, holding him in a full nelson.

Patrick held the machete out in front of him and approached. He placed the sharp tip right at the corner of Kyle's left eye. "One twitch and your eye comes right on out." Kyle held as still as midnight. The blade was heavy, and the tip dug into the corner of his eye. He felt something warm and wet slide down his cheek, and he didn't know if it was a tear or if it was blood.

"Do it," Scotty said. His voice was different now. Husky and focused. "Take the spy's eye out. Take it right the hell on out."

Kyle knew that all of this was designed to put a good solid scare into him, that kids didn't kill or maim other kids, but there was something in Scotty's voice that told him that yes, actually, sometimes kids really did kill or maim or even blind other kids. That a kind of bloodlust sometimes infected them, and they did things they would have to bury and hide later when good sense came back to them.

"I'll eat it," Scotty said, looking to Patrick for approval. "Pop it out and I'll eat it. Swear to God." Then Scotty tittered. A jungle sound that could only come from a very dark place.

Patrick must have sensed how bad this could turn, and Kyle was relieved to feel him try and pull it back a little. "You're a sick boy, Clonts. I believe you just would do that." Patrick withdrew the machete. "Problem is, he's already seen our stash, so taking out his eyes won't do us any good." Patrick put his hands on his hips and thought what to do. Joel released the nelson, and Kyle slumped forward—a single ball trapped inside a triangular pool-rack. "Look," Patrick said. "Look at the faggot crying."

Kyle was relieved to know that it wasn't blood flowing down his cheek, but he didn't understand the word *faggot*. He was pretty sure it meant the same thing as *queer*. "Are you a faggot?" Patrick asked him. Kyle didn't know what to say or do, so he stood there mute. Patrick reached out lightning fast. The sound of the slap across his face was loud in the woods. "I asked you a question. You a faggot?"

Kyle didn't want to answer wrong, so he still didn't answer either way. The slap came again. The tears were flowing down his face now, dripping into the earth. No one had ever done violence to him before. Daddy had spanked him with his belt, and Mama had gotten him lots of times with a switch to his legs. But this was entirely different. An answer was demanded, so Kyle nodded his head.

"I knew it! I just knew it! A faggot. You want some dick, faggot? You hungry for my pecker?" Patrick dropped the machete to the ground and his hands went to the front of his jeans. And Kyle sensed a new, equally evil, turn of course. "Think he's hungry for it?"

"Hell yeah," Scotty said. "Look at 'im. He's droolin' for it. Jeez, I ain't ever seen a for-real queer before."

Joel Sewell just stood there looking into the woods, his face a mute horror.

Patrick's blue jeans and underwear were down, stretched tight across his pale thighs. His penis was a tiny mushroom poking through a sparse tangle of red/orange hair. "Touch it," he said. "Crawl on over here and touch it." Kyle didn't move. The bramble of red pubic hair was disturbing and foreign to him. He wanted only to be far away from here.

"Touch it," Patrick said. "Kiss it." He sidled over to Kyle, waggling his tiny penis between thumb and forefinger. Kyle turned his head as far away as was physically possible. "And if you ever tell what you seen here today, I'm going to ram it up your ass." Patrick rubbed his sex organ through Kyle's hair, then along the outside of his ear.

Scotty giggled. It was the wild jungle titter again.

Joel still looked away, seemingly refusing to watch. *He probably saw enough ugliness in the mirror every morning to last a lifetime*, Kyle thought.

And he knew they were all back in the dark place where anything could happen.

Patrick then stood directly in front of Kyle and shoved his pants all the way down to his ankles, his penis twitching and growing.

"Touch it. Last chance, then I really will pop out your eye."

Kyle saw no way out of this. He was trapped. There was no choice. He reached out, hand open, hesitant at first. "Lookit, the fag's going after my pecker. Look, Scotty. Lookit 'im. Really is a faggot."

"A real live faggot."

Kyle's hand inched forward. *What choice did he have?* He had no choice. He closed his eyes and did it. He grabbed hold of Patrick Sewell's sad little balls and squeezed them hard enough to pulverize stone.

Kyle was on his feet and running before Patrick Sewell even hit the ground.

KYLE FIGURED TO SCRAMBLE RIGHT PAST
Joel and take off into the woods. But Joel reached out—almost like
a reflex—and hooked Kyle by the collar. Before Kyle could comprehend that he had not in fact escaped, Joel had him back in a full
nelson, locked down tight.

Patrick was on the ground curled up into a ball, pants around
his ankles. Joel maintained his hold on Kyle, and Scotty was waiting for instruction of what to do next. They all watched Patrick
rock his body back and forth to soothe the pain, until finally he
uncurled himself and pulled up his underwear and pants. Still on
the ground, Patrick crawled for the machete. And when he looked
up at Kyle, there was no question as to what was going to happen
next. He saw murder in Patrick's eyes. They all saw it. And then
Kyle felt Joel Sewell relax his arms. Nobody else could tell, but Joel
was letting him go. Joel must have seen that thing in his brother's
eyes that he knew could only be extinguished with blood. Kyle
slipped out of the loose full nelson and took off.

Scotty was reaching down to help Patrick up, and that gave Kyle a little bit of a head start.

Kyle ran for all he was worth, speeding through the woods, just praying that he was heading in the right direction. He must have been, because quicker than he thought, he could see bright sunlight ahead where the woods gave way to Sweetwater Creek. Kyle rocketed himself up and over the bank. He landed hard. Then a quick scramble right into the cave.

Jason and Wade were back in there. Jason was poking the fire, and Wade was back in the shadows, digging, with candles flickering around him. "How'd you find this place?" Jason asked. There was anger in his voice. "Did you follow us? I told you what spying would get you."

Kyle thought about how he could explain everything that had happened, but he saw Jason look up when he heard running feet vibrating the ground overhead. Jason looked past him, over his shoulder. Kyle turned around and saw Scotty, and then Joel dropping past the mouth of the cave like poisonous spiders. Patrick followed behind, and the three of them climbed into the cave like they owned it. Patrick was grimacing, still in pain, but his anger was driving him now. He held his machete in one hand. Patrick walked up to Kyle and struck Kyle's mouth with his fist. Kyle's bottom lip split open and he could taste the blood. For some reason, it didn't hurt much at all. The pain wouldn't set in until the next day.

"What's going on here?" Jason asked.

Patrick grabbed Kyle by the neck of his shirt and pulled him close. "This is between me and him," Patrick said. "He knows what he done."

Jason was calm, his tone reasonable. "What did he do, Patrick?"

"He knows."

"Knows what?"

"Spying. He was spying on us."

"Spying? Spying?" Jason contemplated this. "Spies have to be taught a lesson." Kyle's world grew dark. His brothers were going to help Patrick punish him. "You know what they did to spies in the War?"

"You're goddamn right I know. And we're going to teach him a lesson."

"I reckon he earned it," Jason said and turned his back on them. Patrick had started dragging Kyle out of the cave when Jason turned back around. "How'd he track you?"

Patrick stopped. "What do you mean?"

"How did Kyle track you through the woods?"

"How'm I supposed to know that?"

"Well, it's just that he ain't but ten. How'd you let some little kid track you through the woods? If I was you, I'd be a little embarrassed about that. It don't reflect well on you."

"Shut up, Edwards." Patrick raised the machete to Kyle's throat. "I know how you are with words. Tricking people. You can't trick me."

"Ain't trying to trick nobody, Patrick. Just saying, he ain't but a little kid. You don't need that long knife to hold no little kid. I ain't trying to stop you. You can take him."

"You're goddamn right I—"

The popping sound, the little mini-explosion, came from the back of the cave. They all looked and Wade was standing there with a candle in one hand and a spoke gun in the other. Then Patrick was screaming. There was a tiny hole punched in his right cheek. No blood, just a little black hole from the BB or pebble or whatever Wade had packed into the spoke gun. Patrick let go of Kyle and dropped the machete, both of his hands going to his face, covering it. Then they saw that the blood did begin to flow, trickling from under his palms. Patrick made a chewing motion with his mouth, then spit something onto the ground. It was a BB.

Jason had already grabbed an armload of the bloodweed javelins. He broke one in half and rubbed the milky crimson sap under his eye like Indian war paint. Then he started throwing them, sending them out like fighter planes. One pierced Scotty's chest, a bloom of blood unfurling on his Judas Priest T-shirt. Joel was already gone. Patrick was right behind him, running, hand covering his cheek. Scotty paused long enough to break the bloodweed across his knee and shoot them the bird, then turned and kept running.

Kyle was dazed. Not because of what had happened, but because his brothers had defended him.

AFTER INSPECTING THE ROAD AND FIND-
ing no trace of the injured woman or her overturned car, Kyle
pedaled back to the house, still careful of his Sunday clothes.

Nobody liked going to church. It was Mama mostly who made
them do it, and she seemed to like it least of all. It was hard on
her to get all of the kids up and cleaned and dressed and fed. And
on top of that, get a pork roast in the oven so it could cook slow
and be ready when they got back home. Daddy never helped her;
he just stayed down in the basement a lot, working on projects
Kyle never saw the fruits of.

All the boys hated the clothes they had to wear. The shiny
black shoes were stiff and pinched your feet. The button-down
shirts were scratchy against their skin, and the polyester suit jackets smothered them. And the knotted ties (Kyle's was a clip-on)
choked them so that it seemed like drawing a breath was a struggle
and their heads felt hot and puffy from the circulation being
slowed down. It was awful.

They would all line up and file into Daddy's car, Mama standing there like an attendant, wetting her thumb with spit to rub off any grease or dirt they had managed to get on their faces since getting dressed. Nobody ever spoke in the car on the ride to church. Kyle guessed they were all too busy trying to draw a breath and unpinch their toes.

Sunday School was first—even for Mama and Daddy. The kids were split up based on their age and there was a men's group and a women's group for the parents. Sunday School wasn't too bad. The teacher would let them cut up some, and she told them some of the more interesting stories from the Bible—like Noah and the great flood, how Jesus rose zombie-like from the dead, and stuff about lepers whose noses and arms would just rot off and people killing each other with rocks. Just the good stuff.

The church service was another matter. It never lasted less than two hours. Two hours was two weeks in kid-time. The congregation would sort of wander in like dazed disaster victims while an old lady played spooky music on the organ. The organ lady had white hair done up in a perm and a henna rinse that made it look white and purple at the same time. The Edwardses would all sit together on one of the long wooden pews. The pews seemed to have been built of the hardest wood available, and constructed so that no matter how you fidgeted, you couldn't find a comfortable spot. And fidget Kyle did, because there was nothing else he could do. He had to sit there for two hours in clothes that poked and grabbed and scratched him, perched on a bench that tormented his backside, and listen to Preacher Seevers yell and scream and sometimes even speak in tongues.

It was funny, because Preacher Seevers always started his sermons in the most reasonable and calm tone of voice. He would talk to them like they were all sitting down to supper and he was just telling them a story to pass the time. The story always seemed to be about a man who had gotten off on the wrong path. Sometimes he was a man who struggled to do good, but made a bad decision. Usually, it was TEMPTATION that had caused the man to take a drink, or lay out from church. Or steal money, or lust after his friend's wife. TEMPTATION could cause a man to do any number of vile and evil things. And God always—always—punished those who gave in to TEMPTATION.

By the time Preacher Seevers got to whatever it was that was tempting the man, that was when his voice took on a tone of urgency. That was when a light sheen of sweat would gloss his forehead and his gestures at the podium would become broader and more animated. By the time the man in the story was wallowing in whatever sin TEMPTATION had led him into, Preacher Seevers would be screaming at them, the calm friendly man who had started the sermon was long gone, and in a voice of full-fledged rage, Preacher Seevers told them just exactly how hot the fires of hell would be, how that fire would first blister and then char their flesh, and how it would burn for an eternity.

The sweat would pour down his face and he would try to stem the flow with his white handkerchief, but it was a losing battle. Engorged veins coursed along his temples, pulsating and standing out in purplish stark contrast to his red, apoplectic face. And spittle would fly from his mouth as he screamed his warnings of damnation at them. Kyle remembered one time when a long cord of saliva flew from the man's mouth, caught on his pointy chin, and then hung from his chin to the tight knot of his tie, and wavered there for a good thirty minutes, just swaying and dangling with his bobbing head, and Kyle just wished like hell that he would wipe it off, but he never did. Finally, it detached from his chin and tumbled down his tie like a Slinky.

About once every month or so, Preacher Seevers would speak in tongues. This was pretty scary. It completely unnerved Kyle, so God only knew how it must have affected a little kid like Grace. The sermon would follow the usual pattern: friendly banter, gradually growing sterner, the appearance of TEMPTATION, leading into yelling and bulging veins and flying slobber. Kyle could usually tell when the man was going to take it all the way and speak in tongues. It had something to do with the slobber. There was less of it.

Instead of flying around in great long ropes, the slobber would gather at the corners of Preacher Seevers mouth in tight, hard, little white pellets. That was the telltale sign. Then all the red in his face would sort of drain to a spot high up on his forehead, and his eyes would roll up in his head. His words would get real quiet, and Kyle could tell he had gone into a kind of trance, and Preacher Seevers wasn't really there anymore. He would start talking in a kind of mumble, but real fast. Kyle couldn't understand it. And the way the man's eyes were set back in his head, all you could see was an opaque milky white. It didn't last but about thirty seconds, then he would fall down to his knees and come back to himself. That usually ended the sermon, because Kyle could tell he was real tired after all that. It took something out of him.

Sometimes the sermon would end with witnessing. Preacher Seevers would whip everybody into a frenzy and he would call for witnesses. If you felt the Holy Spirit in you, if the Holy Spirit had entered you and taken you over, you were supposed to walk to the front of the church and Preacher Seevers would anoint your head with oil. The preacher would call to the congregation, "Come on up, if you feel it. If you feel The Lord in your heart! Do you feel Him? Has He entered you? Then rejoice! I feel Him. He's here with us right now. Is He in you? If He's in you, then come forward. Witness for The Lord. Witness for The Lord!"

And folks would start drifting up. To Kyle, they looked like they were in some kind of trance, like they had been charmed. They kind of lumbered real slow to the front, like they were wading through waist-high water. They held their arms and legs stiff, and looked off into the distance, their eyes out of focus like robots or zombies. He reckoned The Lord really had entered them and taken them over. When they got to the front, Preacher Seevers would dunk his thumb in a little metal pot of oil, and smear their foreheads, vicious like. And when he did that, they would fall to their knees, and after a minute they would get back up and walk back to their seats, like they were normal people again.

Neither Mama nor Daddy ever got up and witnessed. Kyle wanted to know what those people were feeling that would make them act like that. It was like they were not themselves, but that another force had taken over their bodies and made them walk to the front. It looked to him like they had no choice in the matter. Even though he was scared, sometimes Kyle wished The Lord would enter him and make his body walk to the front and get anointed, but He never did. Sometimes Kyle thought about just pretending like he had been taken over, but he never got up enough nerve to do that either.

His favorite part of church, the only part that he truly enjoyed, was the baptism ceremonies. There was a baptism chamber built into the wall up behind the pulpit, and it was hidden behind long curtains. It would be real quiet in the church except for the purple-haired lady playing that spook-show organ music real low. Kyle guessed someone signaled her somehow, and right after the low organ chords stopped, the curtains hiding the baptism chamber would sweep open, and there Preacher Seevers would be, wearing a purple robe and standing waist-deep in clear water. The bottom half of the retaining wall was plate glass, so you could see him standing in the water. It was just like looking at an aquarium built into a wall. After a minute, the organ music would start back up real low and the first person would step down the tile steps and wade over to Preacher Seevers. They would always be wearing a purple robe too.

"Moreover, brethren, I declare unto you the gospel which I preached unto you, which also ye have received, and wherein ye stand; By which also ye are saved, if ye keep in memory what I preached unto you, unless ye have believed in vain. For I delivered unto you first of all that which I also received, how that Christ died for our sins according to the scriptures; and that he was buried, and that he rose again the third day according to the scriptures. Do you accept Jesus Christ into your heart as the Son of God, and as your own personal savior?"

"I do."

Lots of times Preacher Seevers would pinch the person's nose shut for them, then kind of cradle the back of their head, and dunk them in the water good and deep. It looked like a lot of fun to Kyle, and he wanted very much to be baptized. He never was though. His Mama and Daddy were divorced before he was old enough to say that Jesus Christ was his personal savior and really believe it in his heart.

AFTER CHURCH, THE EDWARDS FAMILY went home for a Sunday supper that served as lunch and dinner. For some reason, food never did taste right on Sundays. It never tasted as good as it did the other days of the week. Even when they had leftovers the next day—the exact same food seemed to have more flavor. On Sundays, it tasted flat. Maybe it was because Mama wouldn't let them change clothes until after they ate. That Sunday in July, the day after Kyle made the woman wreck her car, Mama had made a pork roast, some greens, creamed corn with fried okra, corn bread, and banana pudding for dessert.

They were all sitting at the redwood picnic table (it was actually plywood painted to look like redwood) eating their supper. Mama put a vinyl tablecloth over it on Sundays. There was a knock at the front door, and Daddy looked at Mama. Mama got up to go see who it was. All the children turned to watch—they could see the front door from the kitchen eating area.

They all saw that it was a colored lady in a policeman's uniform. Mama talked to her for a minute but didn't let her inside. Kyle knew exactly what the woman wanted. She was coming for him, and in a minute his mama would open the door wide and turn and point back at Kyle and say, "That's him right there. He's the one you want. He killed that woman."

But Mama didn't let the woman in. Kyle saw her looking past Mama, looking at all of them sitting there eating. The woman's eyes caught Kyle's eyes, and he looked away immediately. But it wasn't fast enough. In that split second when their eyes met, it felt to Kyle like they communicated with each other. It felt like he could hear her voice in his head, and her voice said, "You did it. I know you're the one who did it. I can see right through you." And Kyle felt like she could hear his voice in her head, and his voice said to her, "Yes, ma'am, it was me. I did it. I killed that woman. It was me. And I know you have to take me away, and I understand. I don't hold it against you."

The police lady handed Mama a picture. Kyle couldn't see the picture, but he didn't need to. Mama studied it for a minute, then handed it back and shook her head. Then the woman asked Mama another question. Mama turned back to all of them and said, "Boyd, do you ever remember anybody getting in a wreck up on the road?"

Daddy didn't look up from his dinner, just shook his head.

Mama closed the door and sat back down. Daddy raised his eyebrows at her. "They're looking for a girl went missing. Lived right up yonder off of Lee Road. Right pretty girl too."

Daddy got up from the table and went to the front window. He parted the curtain a little bit and watched the police lady leave.

Now she truly was the reticulated woman.

Her mind hadn't cracked, but rather it had expanded into a fibrous network that had to be traversed slowly—lest she fell from the safety of her brain's webbing into one of the empty spaces. She knew that if she fell, fell in her mind, all would be lost. She would be lost. So when she did dare to think coherent thoughts, she was careful to keep her balance while on the relative safety of the interconnected strands of sanity, and not peer into the empty places where the webbing dropped away.

The empty places of her reticulated mind were dark. They held memories. Memories of what the monster had done to her. If she looked, she would remember. And she would slip inside, never to return.

Today, she was allowing herself a certain level of conscious thought. And by "today" she meant *period of wakefulness*. In the course of twenty-four hours, she would experience multiple episodes of wakefulness that she considered days—although she had been here only two actual days. So today, during this segment, she was allowing her mind a level of clarity that she typically deemed too dangerous to allow herself to experience.

The problem with clarity and coherent thought was that they made it impossible to ignore the pain in her body. She had been operating at about 50 percent coherency, and that level allowed her to peer from her eyes like someone squinting through a peephole in a door—the door protecting the person from whatever might be on the other side. But today, this period of wakefulness, the reticulated woman allowed herself to operate at about 80 percent coherency. This would allow her to not only inspect her surroundings, but to draw *implications*. The problem, the drawback of conducting herself at this level, was that the pain in her body could no longer be blocked out. It wasn't that the pain was not endurable, but that because of the nature of it, because of the series of memories it might unleash, the pain might push her off the webbing and back into one of the dark chasms.

Her woman parts. A steady, deep throb. And the crusty, itchy sensation of dried blood. And her throat. The constant burning. The intense fire that churned there. If these things were felt, then her mind could not help but to reflect back on the cause of these injuries. And the cause was there for her to examine if she so chose, but the memory of it was stored outside of the safe network of rational thought, in the empty spaces between. Where the monster lived.

It was dark up here. She only sensed "up." She had no empirical knowledge to base that on, but, nonetheless, she felt that she was "up here." And now, with this level of clarity she was allowing herself, she had an insight. When the monster came, it came from below. Sound. The sound of it approaching told her this. She had made an inference, and that was a higher brain function. And with that, her brain grew less fragmented. A small segment of the web fused together, and her brain grew a tiny bit more complete, more whole.

A chain was cuffed to her left ankle. The chain was anchored to a smooth metal pole. She thought of the pole as home. And a few feet out from the pole, two metal bowls were bolted to the wood floor. Immovable. She lapped food and water from them. There was nothing else in her world, only darkness, so the one object in the center of that would quite naturally become her base, her home.

Today, she ventured out from the pole. Explored. Tentatively at first, careful to feel and sense with her still damaged fingertips for danger. But nothing was there. She extended herself from the pole as far as the chain would allow. She completed a 360-degree circuit, but nothing was there, so she retreated back to her pole. Then she crawled forward again. She lay on her belly (mindful of the sharp uptake in the internal throbbing when she exerted herself this way). From this supine position, she reached out, but still felt only nothingness. She stretched her body outward, every joint and sinew extending to its limits, the shackle biting thoughtlessly into her ankle, and her straining fingers felt something. She felt a surface of some kind. A wall? She decided to call it a wall. It was cool and slick. Her outstretched fingers could just glance it. She had no fingernails, and her fingertips were exceptionally painful from whatever had happened to them, exquisitely sensitive. If she surged forward, she could gain perhaps an eighth of an inch to her reach. When she did this, the wall made a sound. A tiny crinkle sound. Like plastic. If she had her fingernails, she would be able to feel and sense so much more.

After careful exploration, she discovered three such places where she could touch the wall. In the last of these places, there was something different about the wall. She could feel a flaw. A vertical edge. *A seam.* Yes, a seam. All of the stretching had loosened her body somewhat, and where she had at first been able to only feel the wall in scratching glances of her fingertips, she could now maintain light contact with the very tips of her nailless, sensitive fingers. So she rested her finger at the seam. It made a light scratching sound when she flicked it. And there was a sensation that the seam lifted a bit when she did this. She felt certain that when (or if) her fingernails grew back or the pain receded, she could begin to pry the seam apart.

Below, she heard a noise. A creaking door. Then the sharp hollow sound of a boot striking a wooden step. It sounded like a match striking sandpaper. Again. And again. And again.

Like a spider, the woman scuttled to a far corner of her reticulated mind and waited there out of sight. She would emerge again later.

THE
PARALYZED
MAN

KENNY AHEARN SAT ON HIS PORCH AND watched the boy and girl playing in the cornfield. Kenny's eyes were squinted against the bright day, and although he wasn't aware of it, the slitted eyes and his mostly bald head gave him a distinctively reptilian appearance. A nice breeze blew across the porch and it felt good on his head where pinpoint dots of sweat glistened. The breeze licked the sweat away, cooling him, and lifting the few long, wispy clumps of white hair that held on there like recalcitrant weeds. The wind gusted and the lengthy patches of old-man hair were lifted up, writhing around his head, Medusa-like.

Kenny's tongue darted out to moisten his dry lips, and his heavy, doughy hand made a clumsy pass across his head to flatten down the scattered strands of hair. He licked his lips once more and watched the children.

He was in that place again. Maybe that was what was giving him the reptilian appearance. He was in that place that was primordial, where his thoughts were no-thoughts, where his thoughts were lizardly, encompassing everything and nothing simultaneously. Like an atavistic predator he kept his eyes open, but saw nothing consciously. Waiting until something entered his environment and pierced the eye-brain barrier of cognizance, and went straight to the primitive constructions deep within his mind.

The children had registered there. He licked his lips.

Kenny was a deacon at the Lithia Springs First Baptist Church of God. At least he had been before the stroke. It was always something. First he'd come down with the diabetes, had to take them shots, then the stroke had paralyzed the right side of his body. He still could be a deacon of course, using his wheelchair to navigate the wide aisles between the rows of pews, keeping a careful (but nonjudgmental) eye on the flock, being sure they were forthcoming with the tithes in the silver-plated collection plate, not shortchanging The Lord.

Managing the heavy tray used to distribute the grape juice (Kool-Aid in reality) that represented the wine that symbolized the blood of Christ would be too great of a challenge, but he could still easily hand out the wafers (Ritz crackers broken into quarters) that represented Christ's flesh. (Privately, Kenny always thought the idea of symbolically consuming the flesh and blood of Christ was like that movie *Night of the Living Dead*, but he would never in a million years give voice to such a thought.) Since his stroke, he was no longer expected to carry out such duties. His generation was of a time that those with disabilities were to be waited on and not expected to have responsibilities. It was the Christian thing to do.

While he was still in Parkway Medical Center, the congregation had taken up a donation and purchased Kenny an electric wheelchair. Kenny had not known that such a thing existed. The battery on it looked like it weighed seventy-five pounds and had to be recharged nightly, but it ran like a champ.

A group of the church men (including Preacher Seevers himself) showed up the day before he got out of the hospital with a truckload of lumber and constructed a gently sloping wooden ramp from the front porch to the driveway.

And the church ladies delighted in bringing him casseroles of tuna, hamburger, and pork. Enough time had passed now that most of the ladies had stopped dropping off their kitchen creations. Except Opal Phillips. Opal still kept Kenny on her regular rotation of visiting the infirm and crippled. She seemed to have an internal calculator of exactly how many full meals Kenny would be able to meter from each single-dish conglomeration, and would, without deviation, show up the following day with a new casserole.

But there was something about Opal Phillips that set Kenny's teeth on edge. Made his mouth go dry. Mostly, it was the longing looks. At first those longing looks had been spiritual in nature, and Kenny had been content to oblige them. It quickly grew evident that Opal had more on her mind than spiritual communion. The supposedly chaste kisses to his forehead lingered a little too long. It caused Kenny a great deal of anxiety. Invariably, after Opal left, Kenny's mouth had gone so dry that he had to clean hard white balls of spittle from the corners of his mouth.

Other than Opal, the church folks had mostly forgotten about Kenny now. It didn't take long. It was as if that by buying the chair, building the ramp, and delivering some meals they now felt free to compartmentalize Kenny away from their everyday world. He was taken care of, so now they could go on about their real lives.

Kenny wasn't even expected to attend church anymore. And he liked that just fine.

All Kenny had ever really wanted was to be left alone. He'd been that way his whole life, but had never had the courage to give in to his natural personality. He just wanted to be left alone and allowed to retreat into his lizard mind. He didn't blame the awakening of his primordial self on the stroke; it had always been there, even before his mama had passed. But he'd kept it shut away, only allowing himself to dabble in it on occasion.

Up until now, Kenny Ahearn's life had been about cultivating the persona of Kenny Ahearn—building him piece by piece like a playwright creating a character for the stage. The character of Kenny that Kenny had created was a low-key figure. Likeable, but forgettable. He owned his own tow truck and built Kenny's Towing around it. It was a masculine profession. And of course he was a church deacon—a position of negligible importance in the church, but expected as a man reached a certain age. And he did good deeds within the church, serving the community, but nothing that would draw undue attention. Yes, he'd visited his own fair share of the lame and enfeebled.

He'd never married or fathered children, but in this part of the South, there were always certain men who lived with their widowed mothers long into adulthood. It was a cultural stereotype.

But all that was behind him now. There'd be no more Kenny's Towing. Now he'd be drawing a disability check every month. No more going to church and praying for other people. Now they'd be praying for him. The stroke had cost him the use of half his body, but it had freed him of all those artificial roles society expected him to play out. Now society expected him to be nothing more than a cripple, someone they could bring casseroles to and then forget. Which was fine by him. Yes sir. He'd never really wanted to play those parts. Never actually wanted to drive a tow truck. And, truth be told, he hadn't shed a tear when Mama had died. They could do the good deeds within the community their own selves. He'd never wanted any of it.

And, more than anything else, Kenny had never wanted to be a fucking deacon in the fucking church in the first fucking place.

Kenny Ahearn sighed contentedly and licked his lips.

A FALLOW FIELD CHOKED WITH WEEDS, long tendrils of morning glory, towering stalks of polk salad, and hard tufts of crabgrass buffered the stretch of woods behind their house. Grace and Kyle played there sometimes, digging holes and marking them for the treasure hunt game. And it was a good spot for starting fires.

They were both fascinated by fire.

It had been about a month since the woman's car had flipped over on Eden Road. The police lady had not come back in all that time, so Kyle had put the event out of his mind. He had decided that someone must have come along and helped the woman turn her car back over, and probably she had not been hurt as bad as it looked.

This day Kyle took a single kitchen match from the cabinet over the stove. It was the strike-anywhere kind with a fat red phosphorus head. It was late summer, and the weed-covered field was baked dry, the dirt hard as rock, the dense weeds were dead and straw-like. There was a pretty good breeze blowing, so, shoulder-to-shoulder, they hunched over the match and struck it on a rock.

Mama had been in the basement hunting for something when he took the match. He'd seen her come back up carrying three boxes of Mason jars, and pulling her pressure cooker from under the cabinet. Kyle knew that she would be in the kitchen the rest of the day canning green beans or pickling okra or putting up muscadine jelly. So this was their one match, their single opportunity to play with fire.

They went to the farthest corner of the field, out of sight in case Mama looked out the kitchen window. They scooped out a hole as best they could and hunted up some rocks and built up a stone ring to hold the fire. Their bodies formed a little cave over the pit. Kyle struck the match, and it flared beautifully into life—the flame piercing their eyes and awakening something ancient in their minds. The sulfur smell stung in their noses. Once the phosphorus died down and it was just the wood stick burning, a gust of hot wind snuck through their body barrier, and the flame flickered. Kyle was sure it had gone out. But they pressed their bodies together even harder and hunched down a little tighter, and the flame sprang back up, licking the wood. With the utmost care, Kyle lowered the burning match down to the little pyramid of dry leaves, straw grass, and tiny twigs.

The kindling took immediately and Kyle and Grace rocked back away from it as the fire leapt up.

THEY TOOK THEIR TIME ADDING TO IT, growing it. It was fun adding progressively bigger sticks, careful not to put on too much at one time. Once the fire was going good with a solid bed of coals, they started finding different things to burn. They found some red berries in the woods that would at first sizzle then blow open when the heat caused gases inside them to rapidly expand.

With Wonder Woman in one hand, Grace raced back into the woods and found a whole bough that drooped with the berries. Kyle was the Fire Master, so she presented him with the heavy cluster of berries. First he added some more sticks to the fire and got the flames roaring high. He held the berries out, putting them in the heart of the dancing flames. They sizzled like Chinese noodles, then turned black. Then, like a string of firecrackers, the berries exploded—bam-bam-bam-bam-bam-bam. Grace and Kyle both screamed—not from the little explosions, but because the scalding hot berry pulp struck them like shrapnel.

Kyle wasn't wearing shoes or a shirt, so the exploding pulp caught him full in the chest. And each hit hurt bad, like a bee sting. But he couldn't stop to inspect his wounds. Grace was screaming. His first thought was that her piercing cry would carry to Mama in the house and she'd come out to find out what had happened. In his mind, he saw Mama furious that he'd gotten Grace hurt and sending him to the crape myrtle tree in the front yard to pick out his own switch for the whipping that would leave raised red welts on the tender backs of his legs. Mama would be so mad, she might not stop until the welts beaded with blood. So, it wasn't altruism that propelled Kyle to disregard his own wounds and tend to Grace's first.

Grace had both hands cupped to her face, screaming bloody murder so loud it hurt his ears. Kyle pulled her to him, cradling her head against his chest. He soothed her with a long sonorous shushing sound right into her ear, "Shhhhhhhhhh . . . Shhhhhhhhhhh . . . Shhhhhhhhhhhhh. . . ." He stroked her long brown hair and held her tight as he could. And before long Kyle felt some of the tension leave her body. She started moaning in a baby voice, "I want Mama. I want Mama. I want Mamaaaaaaa." This sounded bad. If he had to, he'd take her to Mama, but he wanted to see for himself first.

"Let me see," he said. "Let me look at it." Gentle, Kyle pulled her hands away from her face and looked. It wasn't bad. There were three pinprick burn marks in a short diagonal. One at the scalp line, then in the middle of her forehead, and one right at the corner of her eye. The red spots were already fading. They didn't look any worse than mosquito bites. And that's what they would say they were if asked. The one at the corner of her eye scared him.

Mama was always warning them not to do certain things because
they might put out an eye, and this certainly looked like it could
have put out an eye. But it hadn't, and the physical damage could
be explained away. They were safe.

His chest was a different story. Kyle had been standing a lot
closer to the fire than Grace, so the scalding berry flesh had been
hotter when it hit him, and there was a lot more of it. They both
looked at his torso. Kyle's belly and chest were covered in raised
red dots. And each dot stung like an ant bite. He looked a lot like
he had the year before when he had a bad case of the chicken pox.
He wouldn't be able to explain this. But his face was unmarred. It
was all on his chest and belly. Kyle knew all he had to do was keep
himself covered, be careful not to undress in front of Mama, and
she'd never know. He was safe. They had managed to do something very stupid, get themselves hurt in the process, but not have
to suffer their mama's wrath.

This took away some of their enthusiasm for experimenting
with the fire. They just sat there, hurt, and glad they weren't hurt
any worse than what they were. After a while, Kyle picked up a
pinecone and tossed it onto the ashy embers. It smoked a minute,
then caught fire, the pinesap acting as an accelerant. Then Grace
saw a seedpod from a magnolia tree and threw it on the fire, but
it didn't burn so good. Then she got to looking around for something that would burn better. Kyle too. And soon they were right
back in it, their wounds just fading memories.

Kyle found a plastic milk jug mostly buried in the dirt. He dug
it up and held it out to the fire. The jug blackened then bubbled
then burned. It was amazing. The plastic drooped and elasticized.
A poisonous smelling smoke stung his nose. Green flames took

hold of the bubbling plastic. Grace stopped what she was doing to watch. Kyle was, after all, the Fire Master.

The melting plastic started to drip from the burning end. Fat drops of green flame that made laser beam sounds as they fell, that sounded to Kyle like sound effects in a science fiction movie. But the Fire Master had to drop the jug into the fire when the flames raced up toward his hand. They stood over the fire and watched the plastic coalesce into a burning, molten pool. Kyle found a fat stick and stuck it in. He wrapped the burning blob around the end of the stick like spaghetti on a fork. Now he had a stick that dripped sizzling green orbs of fire.

When Kyle wasn't paying attention, a drop of molten plastic landed square on the top of his bare foot in a quarter-size dollop. It stung like the devil and seriously burned his skin—far worse than the berries. He couldn't brush it off. The plastic had seemingly melted right into his skin, hardening immediately. Kyle reached down and pulled it off—taking a goodly layer of flesh with it. It hurt bad, but he was too fascinated with his wand of dripping green fire to stop and appreciate the pain. It was just one more wound he'd have to hide. In fact, Kyle would be hiding this one for months to come. He would have to wear shoes and socks every day to cover it. And every day the burn would seep plasma and plate-lets that would soak into his sock and then harden into a scab. And every night, no matter how carefully he tried, when he took off the sock it would pull off the scab. The wound took three months to heal. And Kyle would have a perfectly round scar on the top of his foot for the rest of his life. But Mama never found out.

Right that moment though, the amazing green liquid fire took prominence over pain. As it got hotter, the flaming green drips progressed into a steady stream and Kyle was able to draw out lines and circles and patterns of fire in the dirt. Grace clutched Wonder Woman and watched him drawing with liquid fire.

All good things come to an end, and eventually the plastic consumed itself. Kyle headed off for the trash cans lined up behind the house to see if he couldn't find another milk jug.

"Kyle!"

"What?"

"Look."

Kyle turned and saw three places where the weeds had caught fire. The fallow field was more or less bare dirt in the little spot they had tramped down and used for playing, but farther out it was clotted with husky stalks, unruly weeds, and assorted undergrowth—most of it dry as bone.

The three little fires didn't worry him too much, but they clearly needed to be dealt with before they grew unmanageable. He went to the farthest one and stamped it out with his bare foot. The next one was too hot for that, so Kyle found a flat rock and stamped it out that way. He went to the third little fire and threw the rock on top of it.

"Kyle, look."

The second fire was still out, but three more fires had sprung up in circumference around it. These were in the denser undergrowth, and the dead dry vegetation caught like it was drenched in kerosene. Kyle smashed the flat rock down on one fire and extinguished it with two good blows, but then he saw what the problem was: The force of the tamping motion and the feathery dryness of the weeds and brambles sent tiny sparks and embers into the air, little emissaries of fire that touched down and repopulated their kind.

"Help me, dammit!" Kyle yelled at Grace. And he thought it must have been the edge of fear in his voice that broke her from her blank staring fascination, and prodded her into action. He was the Fire Master, and if the Fire Master sounded scared, the time for action was at hand.

Grace dropped Wonder Woman and sprang into wild movement, stamping out the little fires. But she didn't understand the nature of the problem like Kyle did. Later, when Kyle learned the story of the Hydra at school, it would have special relevance for him. For every fire that Grace stamped out with her little sandled foot, three more took its place. There was no way to keep ahead of it.

After a few minutes they both just stopped and watched. The field was afire. And it amazed them. They were adrift in a sea of flame, little sorcerers whose magic had gotten away from them. They'd never seen anything like it. And a sense of the deepness of the trouble and level of punishment that Kyle had just created for himself began to dawn. But that sense was soon dwarfed when the strong breeze pushed the fire forward and it jumped the field and took hold in the woods. The towering pine trees caught in no time, their sticky, inflammable sap hissing and screaming in protest. It was a hundred-foot wall of flame, growing by the second. All told, by the end of this day, despite the best efforts of the Douglas County Fire Department, the fire would take out seventy-five acres of trees. Banked by Sweetwater Creek on one side, and Eden Road on the other, the wind pushed it straight to the reservoir.

Even today, when Kyle Edwards says his prayers at night, he thanks God for letting the wind blow northeasterly that day, into the woods, and away from his house and the other houses on Eden Road.

Kyle came to realize that in truth, this was the day that everything changed. That the black path to damnation was paved with ash. It wasn't because of the woman on the road; it was because of the fire. God might have been looking the other way on the day Kyle caused the woman to wreck her car. But not on this day. On this day God was watching. He saw. On this day, He took notice.

On this day, the Fire Master became Servant of the Ash.

He was not able to bring himself to comprehend any sense of punishment, of right and wrong. He knew only that this thing they had done must be hidden. That they must disassociate themselves from it. Deny everything. Kyle scattered the ring of stones he'd built up and used a stick to stir up the ground. He took Grace's hand and ran toward the house, their bodies silhouetted against the conflagration.

They slipped in through the seldom-used front door (he had to use the key under the mat because that door always stayed locked). Mama was still in the kitchen, canning. Kyle could hear the pressure cooker groaning, the glass jars rattling inside it.

They made their way back to the bathroom. Kyle decided that the first step would be to wash the smoke smell off of them. He soaped them both down quick as he could and wiped it off with a damp rag. The rag turned brown, but it was hard to tell if it was from dirt or soot. He looked Grace over. He dabbed some alcohol on the mosquito bites on her forehead—in his mind they were mosquito bites, they had always been mosquito bites. (Kyle already instinctively understood that the key to successful lying was to truly believe your own lies.)

He inspected himself in the mirror. Other than his chicken pox chest and the burned place on top of his foot, he was clear. He shoved their clothes into the hamper. The clothes would hold more of the smoke smell than their skin would. Kyle thought of the fire spreading outside, the world in flames. How long before his mother took notice? He had to hurry, but he took the time to find them both some clothes that came as close as possible to matching what they had put on that morning. If Mama noticed they had changed clothes, that was it. That was all it would take. She was a smart woman.

Kyle opened the bedroom closet and pulled out the Popsicle stick fort that, as he built up stocks of Popsicle sticks, he'd been constructing off and on that summer. He scattered a handful of the flat wood sticks around it on the floor. Kyle took the bottle of Elmer's School Glue and emptied it quick in the toilet. Then he took some toilet paper (it had yellow and blue daisies on it) and swabbed out the inside of the glue bottle as far down as his fingers could reach. He flushed the whole mess away.

Kyle sat Grace down on the floor in her bedroom and shoved a coloring book and a box of crayons in front of her.

"Stay here. Don't come out. No matter what. No matter what."

"I won't, Kyle."

"Nothing happened. Do you understand that?"

"You mean the fire?" she whispered.

"It didn't happen. We didn't have nothin' to do with it."

"Okay."

"Nothin'."

She nodded, glad her part in this was finished. She had already started coloring a picture of Deputy Dawg before Kyle left the room. God bless her. She had already started to believe that nothing had happened.

Kyle made his way down the hall to the kitchen, composing himself. The attic fan rumbled above him, and he thought he could smell smoke it was already pulling into the house. He had to establish himself to Mama. He had to put himself, his normal self, in front of her. Set himself in her mind as something that existed outside the world of fire. Like the kitchen clock, the ceramic rooster on the counter, the paring knife in her hand—he wanted to put himself in her mind as one of those things that surrounded her right now, right this second, that had no association with the fire.

LOUISE EDWARDS LOOKED AT HER BONY
fingers as she rinsed her hands in the kitchen sink. She had lost
thirty pounds since December, when she had finally made up her
mind once and for all that she was going to leave Boyd. There was
no way she could strike out on her own and raise four children, so
she had decided that she would leave Jason and Wade with their
father. They were older now and didn't need a mother as much.
But Grace and Kyle would come with her. They were only seven
and ten, and needed a mother.

Louise had been putting up string beans all afternoon, and she
looked at the rows of jars that she had completed. She looked at
the bushel of okra she had for pickling, sighed, and placed empty
jars in the pressure cooker for scalding. She reached overhead and
pulled down her tin of alum. This would just kill Boyd. He just
wouldn't be able to understand. They were living like old folks.
All he ever wanted to do was read his books or his newspaper or
mess around in the basement by himself. And after the kids got to

bed, he didn't even want the TV on. It got so quiet that all you could hear was the clock ticking. That clock would just make that single sound over and over and it wouldn't stop and she just wanted to scream sometimes. This was not the life she wanted. She cared for Boyd, loved him even, but she could not live her life like this anymore.

Once a month they took the kids out for dinner and they would go to the McDonald's in Douglasville. That was the big exciting night out for the month. Usually, they didn't even go inside, but went through the new drive-through and sat and ate in the parking lot. One time after begging and begging, Boyd took them out to see a double feature at the Lithia Drive-In Theater up on Highway 78. They put the kids in their pajamas, loaded them up in the car, and saw a movie she couldn't even remember the name of now. Something old that the rest of the world had seen the year before. Burt Reynolds was in it. She fell asleep before the second feature started.

They got married right out of high school. She had been pregnant, but she was pretty sure no one ever knew because she'd caught it early and they'd married within a week. That was just the right thing to do. Nobody in either of their families had ever gotten divorced, but this was 1976 and people got divorced all the time now. But people in Douglas County didn't get divorced all the time. It was a scandal. And people whispered about it for months. This was a Christian county and divorce was not something Christian people did. There were even songs about it on the radio. And people would say that she was splitting up her family. Divorce hurts the children, they said. Jason had been firstborn, and at first she had made up her mind not to have any more, because she didn't believe she could ever love another one as much as she loved Jason. But Wade came along, and of course she loved him equally. And finally she decided she wanted a baby girl and tried again, but she'd gotten another boy, Kyle. And he was the sweetest baby of them all. Just as sweet as he could be. But still, she wanted a daughter to raise, and Grace came along. Louise didn't know if she could find a job making enough money to raise Kyle and Grace on her own. Boyd would have to pay child support. In her heart, she felt that she was being selfish to contemplate this. She was putting her own happiness over her children's. But nobody would ever know how much—

Louise looked up and saw Kyle staring at her from the living room side of the kitchen counter. He looked strange. The look on his face bothered her. She felt that Kyle was somehow able to read her mind. That he had been standing here this whole time listening to her thoughts, listening to her plan out how she was going to break up this family.

"Sugar, are you okay?"

The boy nodded.

"What are you up to? Do you need something?"

Kyle nodded again and held out the empty glue bottle.

"Already? That stuff costs money."

"Been working on it all day. I'm almost finished now. I let Grace help a little bit."

"That's sweet." Louise turned and walked to the laundry room. She rummaged there for just a moment and came back with a new bottle of Elmer's for Kyle.

"Kyle, are you happy? I mean, do you like it here? Living here?"

Kyle nodded, but from the look on his face, Louise could tell that he had no idea what his mother was getting at. "Do you want to wash the okry for me?"

Kyle nodded and dumped the okra in the sink. Louise watched her Mason jars, making sure they got hot enough.

Louise thought she smelled smoke, but sometimes when the wind was blowing right, it brought up the char odor from the burning barrel down the yard. Boyd would blame it all on Jeannie from work. Once Grace got started good in school, Louise didn't have anything to fill up her day. She pleaded with Boyd to let her get a job, but he thought a wife was supposed to stay at home. She guessed it was his pride too. That maybe he thought people would suppose he didn't make enough money to support his family without his wife having to work too. Boyd had finally consented, and Louise thought maybe he had seen something in her eyes when she pleaded with him. She thought he might have had some little insight to the desperation she was feeling. That maybe he sensed she was changing somehow. He saw that she was closing up, dying a little bit. And maybe he loved her too and didn't want to see that happen. Some men would. Some men would enjoy seeing their wife's spirit die a little bit. But Louise knew that her changing was a big concern too. That if she took a job it would change her somehow. And Boyd had been right about that. Louise had taken a part-time job at Harris Real Estate in downtown Austell. Her job was just to help the secretary, Jeannie Simmons, to catch up on the filing. Louise had learned a lot from Jeannie. Before she had met Jeannie, Louise did not know that it was possible to have sex without using Vaseline. Boyd just pushed her down on the bed, greased her up like some kind of piece of rusty machinery, and it was all over in about two minutes. Sometimes she would think about what she needed the next day from the store while he was doing it to her.

Jeannie said that wasn't no kind of way to live. She had divorced her husband three years ago and never regretted it even one time. Jeannie didn't have any kids though. Kids made it different. They were the victims. Louise picked up the little basket of hot peppers from the windowsill, but she was too deep in thought to bother to look out the window. Mostly, the peppers were long and skinny and dark green. And hot as fire. Several of them were streaked with yellow, orange, and red. These were the prettiest (and the hottest), and she selected enough of these to drop one into each jar of pickled okra to give it a little extra flavor and make it look pretty should she give any of the finished jars out as gifts. She kept a spool of yellow satin ribbon in the basement that she would use to tie a bow around the ones she did give out as gifts or took over to visit with someone who was sick. Jeannie had never canned string beans, or made bread-and-butter pickles, or put up muscadine preserves, or creamed her own corn, or done any of the things that Louise did so that Boyd could have the kind of wife and family that he wanted. Louise took great pride at her accomplishments in the kitchen, but she could, quite easily, imagine herself living a life in which all of these things were purchased ready-made in the grocery store. Shoot! Why not? And why not marry a man who didn't have to glop her up with petroleum jelly, but took his time and maybe kissed her sometimes too?

She looked at Kyle again, praying he could not read her thoughts, but he had finished rinsing the okra and gone to the living room. He was sitting in front of the TV watching *Hong Kong*

Phooey. The smoke smell was much stronger now. It was making her eyes sting. Something was wrong. Louise rinsed her hands again in the sink and eyed the hissing, rattling pressure cooker with suspicion.

Then she looked out the window and her mouth fell open. The world was on fire.

THEY WERE ALL STANDING IN THE FALLOW field right below their house, and Kyle was asking himself how would he be acting if he'd had nothing to do with the fire, and he tried to act that way.

Most of the people who lived on the road had gathered here. Fire brings people out. Patrick and Joel Sewell and Scotty Clonts were there. Patrick was wearing a white piece of gauze taped to his cheek. Kyle wondered if when he drank water it would squirt out of the tiny hole Wade had put there. Nathan Sewell was there too, wearing a dark blue polyester suit that had to be smothering him, but he was never seen wearing anything other than a suit and maybe that was why he never lost an election. Daddy-Bob and his wife were there. Daddy and Mama. Jason and Wade, and Kyle and Grace. The fire chief. The paralyzed man was there too. Kyle had seen him rolling down the road, then rolling down their driveway like some kind of bug that moves slow but never stops. He even rolled his electric chair down the little rocky slope to be in the field with everyone else. Daddy shook his hand and clapped him on the back. Kyle looked at him a lot, but looked away quick if he thought he was going to look his way.

The field was a black hole, a charred out mess. And it smelled bad. It was plain to anybody with eyes that the fire had started right here. A swath of destruction led from this spot and headed northeast to the woods. They could see the trees burning off in the distance like red exclamation points. The fire chief was explaining that his men couldn't do anything but keep it contained from the south, the road side, and then let it burn itself out at the reservoir. He said that Eden Road to the south and Sweetwater Creek to the north would act as firebreaks. His men would pace the fire and watch for jumps.

"But how did this happen? And why did it start right here in our backyard?"

"Hard to say, ma'am. The fire marshal will be here directly to investigate just that very thing."

"It don't make no damn sense," Daddy said.

"Sir, I've seen more fires than I'd care to, and all I can tell you is that you'd be surprised." The fire chief's gaze fell directly on Kyle. "Boys are drawn to fire, just natural."

Mama pulled Kyle and Grace in closer to her. "These two was both with me all afternoon. Right with me. All afternoon."

The chief shifted his eyes from Kyle to Wade and Jason.

"And Wade and Jason were at the Braves game with their daddy."

Daddy grunted in confirmation, and the chief's penetrating stare traveled past his brothers to Patrick, Joel, and Scotty. Patrick turned his head away. Nathan Sewell cleared his throat, seeming to say that if you accuse Patrick Sewell, you're accusing the county chairman himself.

"You just can't never tell. That burning barrel there." The fire chief pointed past the teenagers to the rusted-out steel barrel choked full with ashes. "It's directly upwind from here. Directly."

"We ain't burned no trash in three days. Maybe four," Daddy said.

"Don't matter. Fire smolders. Embers can stay live for a week or more. Turn through them ashes with a pitch and see if I ain't right. The fire marshal will. A good breeze like we had today? Shoot. It'll kick a spark right out of there."

Kyle heard his daddy grunt, and that grunt quite clearly communicated that he didn't believe a word of it.

"Lightning strikes." The chief went on. "They can come out of nowhere even on a clear day like this. I've seen it happen before."

Kyle's eyes met up with Patrick Sewell's eyes, and he was surprised to see that there was no animosity there. Kyle realized that if the fire had a silver lining, it was that he no longer had reason to fear retribution from Patrick Sewell and his friends for his knowledge of their secret garden. It was just so much ash now.

Kyle saw that the paralyzed man had wandered away from the group a little bit. He heard his electric chair humming and straining and saw it rocking him back and forth when it went over rocks or through little dips in the ground. The man stopped, reached down, and picked something up from under the weeds in a spot that bordered where the fire had started. Kyle saw plain as day what it was. It was Wonder Woman. Grace's doll.

The paralyzed man scooted the doll up under his dead leg,

then he looked back over his shoulder to see if anybody was watching. And he saw Kyle looking at him. And Kyle couldn't turn away. It was like the paralyzed man had charmed him. And he held Kyle with his eyes, charmed him like a snake and had him under his control. He smiled at the boy. It was ugly. As ugly as sin. Then the paralyzed man licked his lips, and Kyle thought he could hear it when his tongue passed over them. It sounded like sandpaper.

WEARING THE RED, WHITE, AND BLUE WONder Woman cape that Mama had bought for her at the Zayre on Austell Road last Halloween, Grace Edwards stepped into her parents' bedroom. The polyester cape rustled as she tiptoed through the room. Grace really just wanted her doll back, but the cape was giving her courage for now.

It was always shadowy and quiet in her parents' bedroom. It felt hallowed to her. It felt like an empty church. The pine floors seemed to absorb any incidental light even though there was more sun coming through the windows since the fire yesterday had burned down all the woods behind the house.

The bed was perfectly made, and Mama's treasured accent pillows—mink on one side, satin on the other—were propped atop the other pillows, at an angle with the corners pointing up. As she did every time she came in this room, Grace stepped carefully to the bed and retrieved one of those special pillows. She stroked the mink for a minute, petted it carefully as though it was alive and her stroking would bring it pleasure. After a while, she puffed out her cheeks and blew into the mink, delighting in the way the fur parted. She was able to draw little designs in the fur with the stream of her breath.

Grace replaced the pillow, being sure to place it exactly as her mother had positioned it, and crept to the dresser on the other side of the room. She stole a glance at her reflection in the mirror, admiring the cape. The bedroom-set, including the dresser, was made of pecan wood, and Mama said it was the most expensive thing she had ever owned. The pecan was dark stained and absorbed light like the pine floors. Grace scanned the top of the dresser, then once again her eyes were drawn up to her own reflection in the dresser mirror. She was a pretty girl. She had dark features, like Jason. She had deep brown eyes set perfectly into her face like almonds turned on their sides. Her hair was straight and long and cut into bangs. It was the same rich, glowing brown as her eyes. Her skin was tan, not pale like Wade and Kyle. She was a pretty girl and she knew she was a pretty girl because people told Mama how pretty she was every time they went out somewhere. But Grace didn't care about being pretty. She just wanted to be a girl and have fun and for Kyle to be her friend.

She found the little chipped china bowl on the dresser top that held Daddy's change. She fingered through it, trying to decide what to take, when she saw the standing liberty silver dollar. It was big and it filled her small hand so that she could not wrap her fingers around it. It covered her palm entirely. Grace grasped the coin tight while she debated with herself. It was a prize. A true prize. But there was just the one. Daddy was very likely to notice it missing. There were a bunch of quarters and a few fifty-cent pieces. She knew that she could safely take a quarter—even two—and it would never be missed. This was different. It was special. But she wanted to impress Kyle.

She kept the coin and crept out of the room.

Back in her bedroom, Grace gathered all of the materials she would need for the treasure hunt game. The silver dollar was special, so she started with the end of the game first. Taking the spool of brown thread that she had snuck out of the drawer of Mama's Singer sewing machine, she began wrapping the coin in thread, over and over, round and round, weaving the thread in places so that it could not unravel, until she was certain that it was secure. She cut the thread, leaving about a foot of excess length. She held it up and examined it. The coin swung back and forth like a pendulum or a watch on a chain.

The next step was the red and white plastic bobber she had taken directly off Daddy's fishing pole propped against the wall in the carport. Daddy would notice that for sure too, but he would blame Wade. Wade was always sneaking off to Sweetwater Reservoir to fish off the banks. Grace tied the bobber to the end of the thread, and she was delighted with the results. She knew her plan would work perfectly. Kyle sometimes said that the treasure hunts Grace orchestrated were baby-cry—too easy. Not this time though.

She gathered little slips of paper and began writing. Sometimes she paused between one slip of paper and the next, thinking, imagining. Then she would smile and scribble down what she had thought up.

Grace ran from the house and set about the work of setting it all up.

KYLE WAS WATCHING TV, CHIN CRADLED in his palms, sitting cross-legged on the floor, about one foot from the pulsing screen. He noted Grace's red, white, and blue cape (he hadn't yet told her what really became of her doll, but would have to soon) as she marched up to him and held out a tightly folded scrap of paper.

She smiled. He smiled.

The game was afoot.

The stench of char and soot was heavy in the air, but for now Kyle put that out of his mind. In the sunlight on the driveway, he unfolded the note and read it again. In Grace's childish scrawl, it said: *Go to the rabbit.* Kyle headed off to the side yard where the rabbit was kept in a hutch their daddy had made from scrap plywood and chicken wire. Maw-Maw Edwards had given the bunny to Wade last Easter, but after a short period of enthrallment, Wade's interest had moved on to other things, and he proclaimed that once the rabbit died he would harvest four lucky rabbit's feet.

The hutch was tucked into a shady spot where the woods began (or used to, before the fire). Kyle first looked all around the exterior of the cage, careful to inspect the bottom. He opened the hutch door and rooted through the dirty, seldom changed straw. Nothing. He picked up the aluminum pie pan that served as a food dish and looked under it. He also inspected the bottom of the tin pan lest anything be taped there. Still nothing.

Grace squirmed with delight. *Not so baby-cry after all*, she thought. She had put a lot of effort into setting up the game and felt that this would be the best one yet.

Kyle folded his arms, seeming to decide that thought should take priority over action. Then it came to him, and he reached back inside the cage and gingerly picked up the rabbit (which was known to bite on occasion), and poked through the straw, which was warm from the rabbit's body. Still nothing. He was pulling his arm from the cage when a glimpse of white caught his eye. There was something peeking out from the mound of dog kibble that they fed the rabbit. Kyle plucked out the note and read it: *Go to the front door.*

At the front door, the next instruction was in the first place he looked—under the welcome mat. This was par for the course: Some were ridiculously easy, while others were fiendishly hard— sometimes dangerous. In block letters, this note urged him to explore the medicine cabinet.

In the bathroom, Kyle inspected all around the outside edges of the medicine cabinet, paying close attention to the bottom in case the next note was taped there. He opened the mirrored front, conscious of seeing his reflection slide away from him. The three enameled metal shelves were clotted with rust stains and jammed with bottles of aspirin, tinctures, half-used tubes of lotions, salves, creams, various laxatives, enema hose tips, Band-Aids, and all of the other things a family finds use for over the years.

Kyle exhaustively looked under and inside each and every item. But he avoided the dark glass bottle of Mercurochrome. Mercurochrome was the curse of Kyle's boyhood. Like most boys, seemingly every new day brought a scraped knee, or a stubbed toe, or a thorn puncture, or a cut from a pocketknife, and again like most boys, Kyle's instinct was to seek out his mother whenever he was hurt. His mother's first aid always began by blowing on the new wound—a steady cooling stream of breath that invariably brought relief. Unfortunately, her second, and likewise invariable response was to reach for the hateful bottle of Mercurochrome.

It came in a small glass bottle, the size of a big man's thumb. The bottle cap had a thin frosted glass wand attached to the bottom, to be used to paint the tincture on open wounds. The Mercurochrome itself was a shocking carmine color, with some orange thrown in, like blood mixed with rust. And it stained the skin this color for days afterward. And it burned like acid. It stung the flesh like a soldering iron. Wherever the little wand painted its bloodred antiseptic, it was like a row of hornet stings, burning, pulsing. So intense was the pain from Mercurochrome that Kyle's aversion to it had finally overridden his inborn instinct to seek out his mother for comfort. Now he hid his hurts from her, and in fact had not had to undergo the red trauma in nearly a year.

With everything else inspected, Kyle finally picked up the small dark bottle. He could not have used more care had he been handling a vial of nitroglycerine. He unscrewed the cap a thread at a time, and sure enough, wrapped around the applicator tip with a bit of Saran Wrap was a tiny slip of paper no bigger than that found in a fortune cookie.

Kyle, who was perched on the bathroom sink, looked down at Grace and realized in that moment that in many ways Grace was far braver than he could ever hope to be. In the course of her life, which would ultimately hold much more pain than it would happiness, Grace would never forget the look in her brother's eyes. It was admiration. Pure, distilled admiration. And maybe even love—that emotion siblings of any age seldom bestow upon one another. Kyle stared at her so long and so hard until finally, Grace had to look away from him.

Before he even thought about touching it, Kyle rinsed the wand under the faucet, until the water ran off it clear for a good long time. He peeled off the note and sat it aside. He went to put the cap back on the glass bottle, but in his success he had grown careless, and he tipped the bottle over. The Mercurochrome splashed down on his bare thigh. Kyle saw the horrid neon splotch spread over his skin like a cancer. He locked his jaw and steeled himself for the massive jolt of pain that would wash over him. But the sensation of the Mercurochrome on his skin was cooling and even pleasant. There was no pain. Because there was no wound for the Mercurochrome to disinfect. Kyle had not anticipated this. And it was a revelation for him. His fear, while rooted in truth, had been so great as to blot out the obvious, the rational.

He cleaned himself up and changed into long pants. He would have to wear long pants for three days until the carmine stain faded away. It looked like a birthmark.

That note sent him to the peanut patch where he searched under the hot sun until he found the next slip of paper wrapped tightly around a plant stalk. Then it was to the barbed wire fence. Then to their daddy's toolbox. To the magnolia tree where a note dangled high up—Grace having used thread and a metal nut for weight to toss it up there. Then a risky, but ultimately successful reconnaissance mission to the white wooden beehives nestled in the far corner of the backyard. (Grace had placed the note while the honeybees were drowsing in the morning stillness, but on her exit, she stood back a distance and struck the box with a hefty rock to wake them up.)

The next instruction gave Kyle pause: *Go to the parlise man mailbox.*

KYLE TREKKED TOWARD THE CORNFIELD with Grace following, her cape flowing behind her. She would be both the judge and impartial observer. He planned to emerge from the corn where it grew right up to the shoulder of Eden Road so that he would be facing the paralyzed man's house. For now, standing safely concealed two rows back, Kyle could see the paralyzed man sitting on his front porch, just staring at nothing. Kyle jutted his arm behind him, motioning with his hand for Grace to approach with quiet care.

The house had been silent and looked empty when Grace had placed the note in the mailbox that morning, otherwise she would not have dared such a maneuver. Even then, she had sat on the other side of the road, concealed in the corn for a good long time. To make sure. And although she had never been entirely sure, never entirely comfortable with this escalation of difficulty and dare in the treasure hunt game, she did it anyway, her instincts telling her that she was leading herself into sure danger. She did it for Kyle. To impress him, to prove to him that she wasn't a baby, that she was deserving of his time and companionship. So she kept her eyes firmly on the mailbox just on the other side of the road. It was decrepit and the metal support post tilted drunkenly to the side like a tombstone heaved by the contractions of ground frost. The mailbox door hung open on rusted hinges like a broken jaw, old yellowed bills and circulars vomiting from it. Grace darted across the road, shoved the note far in the back, and was back hidden in the corn in less than three seconds.

Kyle took another tack. He had to figure out a way to retrieve the note right under the eyes of the paralyzed man. There was no way he would acknowledge defeat, acknowledge that Grace had managed to place the next clue out of his reach. Even if it came down to a blatant dash-and-snatch, he would accomplish the task set before him.

Grace smiled to herself in unspoken admiration as she watched Kyle set up and execute the retrieval.

He circled back through the corn, emerged on the road well above the paralyzed man's house, and began walking at the most leisurely of paces, as though he was maybe heading down the road to Sweetwater Reservoir to go swimming. This route took him directly in front of Patrick and Joel's house—which was next door to the paralyzed man, separated by a plot of pole beans. He saw no sign of the Sewells and was glad for this. Patrick Sewell might not be actively seeking revenge on Kyle, but he likely wouldn't let a golden opportunity to inflict misery pass him by either. It was just his nature.

As he approached, Kyle was very much aware of the paralyzed man's eyes watching him from the sloping, gently warped porch.

As he got directly in front of the house, Kyle made a show of becoming aware that there was a person on the porch.

"Howdy," Kyle said.

The paralyzed man nodded his head in curt acknowledgement, his eyes imperceptible behind slitted lids.

Kyle then made a show of noticing the glut of sales papers, mailers, and grocery flyers advertising MoonPies and ground beef for sixty-nine cents a pound—all toned ochre by the heat, sun, and humidity.

"Sir, would you want me to bring your mail up to you?"

The paralyzed man took his time answering, as though mulling over the pros and cons of such an interaction. Finally, in an agreeable tone, he said, "That would be fine, girl. That would be just fine."

"Sir?"

"Bring it, girl."

"I'm a boy."

"Boy. What I meant to say. Bring it."

Kyle took care in pulling out the mail, and when he spotted the folded note tucked to the rear, he grabbed it quick.

Kyle walked up the snaking wheelchair ramp, carrying the armload of mail, Grace's note palmed like a bribe. The wood ramp still smelled of the chemicals used to treat the lumber, and its newness stood out in dramatic contrast with the uneven planes of the weathered porch.

The paralyzed man motioned to a small, pollen-stained glass-top table and Kyle dumped the mail there. "Mighty nice of you. 'Boy.'"

"It wasn't no problem."

"Y'all them that lives right over yonder?"

"Yessir."

"Two brothers and a little sister?"

"Yessir."

"Yep. I've seen you all. Don't bother nobody."

"Nosir."

"Christian?"

"Yessir."

"'Course you are. Seen you in church." The man paused, reflected, then added, "Not like them that lives right here next door. Sewells. They pose as Christians." The paralyzed man leaned to the side and spat on his porch. "County chairman my eye."

"I don't guess I know them too well," Kyle said.

"Ain't nothing worth knowing about that lot."

"I reckon not."

The paralyzed man said, "You all are good trees. Keep to yourselves."

"Sir?"

"I stutter?"

"No, sir. You said my family is trees."

"People, boy. Good people. Had the stroke, you know."

Kyle nodded and took a polite half step back away from the paralyzed man, a gesture to communicate that he was ready to leave.

"Let me give you a quarter for fetching my mail."

Kyle knew that he could get a whole pack of watermelon Now and Laters at the reservoir bait shop for less than a quarter. A pack of Now and Laters could be rationed to last a whole day if you were disciplined about it. But Kyle's skin had begun to crawl. He wanted off the porch more than he wanted the Now and Laters. He took another half step backward.

"Nosir, I just couldn't take that. I appreciate it, though."

"Just wait a minute and let me reach here in my pocket."

As Kyle shuffled a bit farther away from the man, he saw that one side of the paralyzed man's body worked just fine, while the other side was dead.

"No. Nosir, I've got to—"

The paralyzed man's good left arm shot out like a striking cobra, and his hand clamped down on Kyle's wrist. It was tight and unyielding like metal.

"What you got in your hand there, boy? What you trying to steal from me?"

Kyle tried to wrench his hand free, but the man's grip was powerful. There was no give to it, no question of wriggling free from it.

"Nothin'! I wasn't trying to steal nothin'."

"Open your hand, boy. Open your hand or I swear to God above I'll break it open."

Again, there was no question of refusal. Kyle did as he was told.

The paralyzed man grunted when he saw the small scrap of folded paper in Kyle's palm. "Open it."

Kyle manipulated the slip of paper using the fingers of his free hand. He held it out for the paralyzed man to read.

"'Go to the green pond for your treasure.' *Treasure* is misspelled. What's it supposed to mean?"

"Nothing. It don't mean nothing. It's a game."

"A game? A game? Why, you're playing a game with the devil, son. Do you think I'm stupid? Do you think old Kenny Ahearn ain't right in the head?"

Kyle struggled as best he could. His hand had gone from tingly hot to blood-starved cold, then just numb. He pulled so hard to get away that he pulled the monstrous metal wheelchair forward just a bit.

"Do you think I don't know who you are?" the paralyzed man hissed at Kyle. Kyle could see his yellow teeth dotted with black spots of decay. Drool spilled lazily from one corner of his mouth. "You're them that set that fire. You're the ones. Firebugs. That's you, boy. Firebug."

Kyle surprised himself by saying, "You're crazy. Let me go. Let me go or I'll tell!"

"Kyle! Kyle!"—It was Grace. Kenny Ahearn and Kyle both looked up, their faces almost touching, and saw Grace standing at the road's edge, the cornstalks towering behind her little girl's body. Her cheap patriotic cape stood out in stark, absurd contrast to the verdant background. Grace turned away from them and yelled back into the corn, "Daddy! Daddy! Kyle's right over here!" She turned back to face the boy and the man in the wheelchair on the porch. "Kyle, you better hurry up! Daddy's been looking everywhere for you."

The paralyzed man maintained his constrictor grip on Kyle's wrist for a moment longer, as if to prove that he didn't care if Kyle's daddy was coming or Tecumseh Sherman or Jesus Christ Himself. He held Kyle's eyes with his and said, "Get on up out of here, firebug" and released Kyle's wrist at the same moment that

Kyle was jerking away. Kyle stumbled and fell on his back with a jaw-cracking thud, immediately turning over and scrambling away.

The paralyzed man watched the boy dart across the dirt road and disappear into the corn, then leaned to one side and spat on the porch.

THEIR ENCOUNTER WITH THE PARALYZED
man had cast a pall over the afternoon. They'd had enough trouble to last them a good long time and didn't want any more.

Grace and Kyle made their way through the corn until they got to the barbed wire fence and the cow pasture. Careful to avoid the sharp rusty barbs, Kyle pulled up on the bottom strand to create a gap for Grace to wiggle through on her stomach. Then she held it up for him. Once through, Kyle scanned around for Buddy the bull and spotted him dozing in the shade on the far side. The pasture and the pond were west of the fire, so everything here was unchanged.

By the time they got to the green pond, Kyle was feeling optimistic again. He felt that maybe they were forgiven for setting that fire. That maybe God had given them a warning to start acting right or He would send bad things their way. And it struck Kyle that God was like Mercurochrome, in that He could burn you and hurt you like you'd never been hurt before. But it was for your own good. God's burning stained you and cleaned you out so that you wouldn't be infected by the evil you had wallowed in. But if you kept your soul clean and didn't scrape it and tear it with every bad thing you did, then the Mercurochrome—God's presence—still left its mark on you, but it didn't hurt. It cooled you and felt good.

It was shady and cool at the green pond. The wind played through the hanging branches of the massive weeping willow trees that shielded the pond like a living curtain.

Kyle was ready to get back to the treasure hunt game. He was excited again. He saw the red and white fishing bobber that surely was meant for him, listing in the soupy green pond water. This was going to be the prize, the end of the game.

The pond was small, only about thirty feet across. Which meant that the bobber and whatever treasure that dangled beneath the surface was about fifteen feet from his grasp. The green pond was a special place for them. Jason and Wade knew about it of course, but they seldom came here. It was from here that Grace and Kyle hatched their plans or just sat on the red clay banks throwing rocks into the water. Kyle thought about how he was going to get the floating prize without actually wading into the viscous green water. While the pond was small in circumference, it appeared to be pretty deep. It was not the kind of water you would want to wade into.

He searched about, his mind scrambling for ideas. He thought about finding something that he could maybe use to float himself out there to grab hold of the bobber, but Kyle couldn't imagine what he could use to do that. Then he thought about fishing it out. All he would need would be a stick or a limb long enough to hook the string under the bobber, but he couldn't find one long enough. Kyle knew that if he crossed to the far side of the pasture and into the wood lot, he could find one easy, but that would put Kyle in the bull's line of sight, and he had already had all the adventure he cared for in a single day.

All of the other woods where he might find a good limb were burned to the ground. He looked around, casting about for the obvious, when it hit him. The weeping willows. They were old trees, towering and sturdy. The pendulous branches cascaded downward, encircling the green pond, some dragging the ground. He spotted a good-size branch that extended outward, tapered, and hung down vine-like close to the center of the pond. With his eyes, he traced the branch back to where it sprouted from one of the main limbs and climbed up the tree to reach it. Kyle grabbed hold of the branch and pulled it down with him, bending and pulling it to the bank. He started yanking on it, climbing up it and bouncing—testing it. The branch held him easily and gave no signs of weakness. He looked at Grace to make sure that she appreciated what he was going to attempt. There was a sly little half smile on her lips, and a shine in her eyes.

Holding on to the slender branch, Kyle swung himself over the pond. The first pass didn't get him anywhere near the fishing float. His aim was better the second time, and he swung directly over the bobber, but to pluck it out of the water, Kyle would have to hang on with one hand and reach down with the other. There was no way for him to get low enough to do that without dragging his lower body through the water.

On the bank, Kyle climbed higher up the branch to where it was thicker, then pivoted so that his body flipped upside down, his legs wrapped tight around the thick upper branch. He hung there, not moving, like a sleeping possum.

"Well, push me," he said to Grace.

Her smile grew to full-fledged and she got behind Kyle and pushed, tentative at first, then harder.

Kyle swung out over the pond like a pendulum on the world's biggest clock. His head grew hot and tight from the oscillating force pushing the blood down. The world was upside down and rushing past him too fast to make it out. There was the long green streak of the water, and two short red streaks of the red clay banks. As he grew accustomed to the force and the motion, he could make out the tiny red/white streak of the bobber.

"Not so fast," he said. "Slow me down a little bit."

Grace complied and it all came into a bit sharper focus.

"More. Slow me down some more."

Grace's pushing became the most gentle of nudges and Kyle swung across the pond in a slow, graceful arc.

Trusting the branch and trusting his legs to hold the branch tight, Kyle let his arms hang down freely. The water was just out of reach. He eased his legs just the tiniest bit and shimmied down about a foot. He dared not risk any more than that, as the branch grew skinnier and more fragile toward the tip. It was enough. His fingertips dredged the water. He was swinging so slow now that Grace had to find a stubby branch to extend her reach to keep pushing him. He bided his time and waited for the perfect pass. One. Two. Three. He stretched and plucked the bobber out of the water, the prize, cocooned in brown thread, hung from it like a sinker.

Kyle grinned at Grace in utter triumph, and she was so excited that she jumped up and down. He reveled in his accomplishment for a little bit, and he guessed he was taking pride in it, and remembered Preacher Seevers had said pride was a sin, and he guessed that was true, because God got busy punishing him for that sin. His pendulum movement over the pond had grown so slow that he was no longer swinging close enough to the bank for Grace to reach out and push him. Each pass grew a little slower, settling back into the equilibrium position. He thought about sending Grace to find a stick long enough to prod him with, but by the time she found one, Kyle would be at a standstill, well out of reach. His only chance would be to climb up the branch and into the tree. But first he had to get his body right side up.

He tossed the treasure onto the bank, then set about getting his body positioned upright on the suspended limb. It took three twisting lunges, but Kyle finally managed to bend his torso and grab hold with his hands. He shimmied up the branch, and he was glad it was a good strong branch. It never did break, but the tiny willow leaves started tearing off under his fingers. His tight grip was pulling the leaves loose from the branch, and every time a few leaves would give way like that, he would slide down and would have to tighten his grip, and that, combined with the downward motion, caused more leaves to give way. It was an avalanche effect. It was like holding on to a greased pole. The leaves gave way in a popping cascade and Kyle plunged into the green pond.

It was warm like bathwater. A thick green stew of living organisms enveloped him, held him gently. Kyle had thought the water would be cold, revolting, and lifeless, but it felt good, warm and comforting. He would have stayed down in it, but of course he needed to breathe. Kyle's feet sank into the soft bottom, but found enough resistance to propel him upward. He broke through the surface, green slimy pond scum covering him like a birth caul. He stood up. It wasn't deep at all. The water came to his chest, but the clay bottom continued to give way and he sank farther standing there. Kyle made his way to the bank, the wet clay sucking at his shoes.

Kyle took off his shirt, and Grace let him use her Wonder Woman cape to wipe the slime and algae from his arms, face, and hair—ruining it. He smelled the same way a newborn puppy smells—sharp and pungent, offensive at first, but also familiar and comforting.

Kyle felt different somehow. He had gone through two trials in two days. Fire and water. He was growing, changing, and he knew it. What would be next? What would be his next trial?

"Open it, Kyle. Open it and see if it was worth it."

He unraveled the brown thread. There was so much of it that it gathered in a big puffy pile on his lap. He worked his way down to find the silver dollar piece hidden inside. Kyle stared at the dollar, knowing Grace must have snuck it out of Daddy's room, and he got to thinking about all the mean little things that he had done to Grace over the years—terrorizing her out in the cornfield, calling her a baby-cry, not letting her come with him when he went exploring. Just thinking she wasn't good enough to be his friend. But she had saved Kyle from being trampled and gored to death by Buddy the bull, she had played it perfect and kept quiet about the fire (which had cost her the Wonder Woman doll she so loved), she had saved him from the paralyzed man (Kyle was too overcome with emotion right then to remember that she was the one who had gotten him mixed up with the paralyzed man in the first place), and she had planned and executed the single best game of treasure hunt of his life.

He smiled and hugged Grace. Grace pulled away and looked at Kyle like he had lost his mind. He had never in his lifetime spontaneously hugged Grace. He only did it when Mama made him.

He didn't know what was wrong with him, but Kyle started crying. Tears were a shameful thing to him, and he turned away so that Grace wouldn't see. But she had seen. And that got her to crying too. And they just sat there a minute, crying on the bank of the green pond, neither one of them really knowing why.

"Kyyyyyyyyle!"

Only yesterday he had made up his mind to be better to Grace, to treat her like a friend. And already he had let her down.

"Kyyyyyyyyyle!" The note of alarm in her voice was escalating.

They were in the corn, and he had lost her. The one thing that could completely unnerve her. When Grace reached that level of panic, Kyle typically only had a few minutes to intervene and save her before she broke down in a sobbing spell that could last all afternoon. He hadn't been paying attention.

She could be anywhere among the rows. Kyle had been daydreaming. Thinking about the fire. Thinking about not getting caught. It just somehow didn't seem right to get away with something like that. Like there ought to be a punishment. It was just too big of a thing to have done. Too wrong and bad. Nobody ought to ever be able to get away with doing something that bad. If people were allowed to get away with horrible, dangerous, destructive acts like that, then this world wouldn't be nothing but pure chaos. And he had got to figuring that just because his folks didn't catch him in it, that didn't necessarily mean that he had gotten away with it. Kyle had started to feel like there was something just outside of his field of vision. Something bad. Something that he couldn't quite see but knew was there, hiding itself in the shadows. Biding its time. Maybe God didn't like it when people got away with bad things. And He put the fix in.

Kyle was scared. It was like being chased by a ghost. Or Soap Sally—the crazy woman Mama had told them about who lived off in the woods by herself in a lean-to covered in pine straw. Soap Sally kept a fire burning and she cooked polk salad in a metal pot all day long. That's all she ate. Polk salad (Paw-Paw Edwards used to call it poke sallet) is poisonous, but lots of people eat it. It has to be boiled three times to get all the poison out, but even then, you're still getting some of the poison. All those years of eating polk salad had damaged Soap Sally's brain. She was crazy. Soap Sally had needles on the ends of her fingers. Because her poisoned brain didn't know any better, she jammed sewing needles up under her fingernails, and she would scoop the polk salad right out of the boiling pot using her needle-fingers.

To make money, if Soap Sally ever came across any kids wandering out in the woods, she would get them and stab them with her needle-fingers and boil them in the polk salad and make soap from the fat she rendered off their tender little bodies. And she would sell the soap for money in town to the beauty shops where the women got their hair done and their faces made up. Soap Sally made a lot of money from selling that soap because it made the women's faces smooth and pretty like baby's skin. She told the people at the beauty parlors that she made it from special roots and berries she found out in the woods. Mama said most folks knew it was made out of little kids, but they bought it anyway because of how good it made their faces look.

Kyle realized that he and Grace had burned down Soap Sally's woods. They drove her from her home. Maybe she was living in the corn now. But he was pretty sure Soap Sally was made-up. Just like he was pretty sure that Santa Claus was not for real. Nonetheless, when Christmas came around, Kyle found himself writing letters and composing wish lists and believing with all his heart. And late at night when he couldn't sleep and he could hear branches rubbing and clicking together outside his bedroom window, he thought about how that could be Soap Sally out there, that he could hear her needle-fingers clicking together while she was sneaking around, looking for some kid she could turn into soap and sell in town.

Right now, though, Kyle wasn't worried about Soap Sally. It was the shadows that lingered on the edges of Kyle's world that bothered him. Those shadows were stretching out to him, but when he would turn to look, they'd curl themselves back in like they had never been there. Something bad was coming his way.

"Kyyyyyyyyyyyyle!"

There was something disturbing in Grace's voice that froze his blood, the same way his blood froze when he saw that the fire had gotten away from them. He guessed a part of him always knew that the panic in Grace's voice when she got lost in the corn was at least a little bit playacting. That she was in on the game as much as he was. But there was some new quality to the way she was calling out to him now. The only thing he could compare it to was when they found the fox that had its leg caught up in one of Daddy-Bob's traps and the way it had cried to be set free.

Grace was trapped. Or hurt. Or both.

He took off, tearing through the corn; his hearing tuned like radar to hone in on Grace. Kyle knew it was time for him to pay for the sin he'd committed by setting that fire. Something bad wasn't just coming his way.

Something bad was here.

COUNTY WATER WAS COMING TO EDEN Road.

Kenny Ahearn sat on his front porch and watched the public works crew in their yellow vests as they got to work tearing up the ground. The fine strands of white hair that clung to his otherwise bald head whipped around in the breeze. The men were about a half mile up the street. It didn't make sense to him. He didn't care what they said, there was nothing wrong with the well water. There had been a county meeting last year—Lithia Springs had once been an incorporated city, but that had been dissolved many years ago, and now Lithia Springs was just an unincorporated swatch of Douglas County named for the trace levels of lithium that spiked the water drawn from its natural springs—to vote on whether or not to bring public waterlines to this road. Kenny strongly opposed the idea of losing his free well water and having to pay for the new lines—for many reasons—but he had not attended the meeting to vocalize his opinion, because he did not know if he would be in the minority or the majority, and either way, he did not wish to draw attention to himself. In any case, it came out that the local groundwater was contaminated with chemical runoff from the Watkins Lumber and Pulp Processing Plant in the northern corner of the county. The plant had been fined and shut down until proper waste disposal methods were put in place. The chemical levels were low and said to be harmless in the short term. But it was estimated that it would take fifty years for the groundwater to cleanse itself. It was a public health issue. County water was coming.

Kenny had used his electric wheelchair (God bless the good people of the Lithia Springs First Baptist Church of God!) and gone down to the end of Eden Road that morning and talked to the foreman. Kenny was finding that his wheelchair was opening all kinds of doors for him. Normally, people did not stop what they were doing to make time for Kenny Ahearn. But being in a wheelchair, they seemed to make him priority. Kenny suspected that the sight of a wheelchair made them nervous, and they just wanted to deal with him right away so that he could be dismissed.

The crew foreman had made a big show of hunkering down next to Kenny and telling him how the project would progress. They planned to lay the main line first, starting at the top at Lee Road and working their way down to the bottom where Eden Road met Mount Vernon Road and Sweetwater Reservoir. They would then come back and run pipe from the main line to each house one at a time. There were only twelve houses on the road, and the foreman figured that they would be hooking up Kenny's house in four, five days at the most.

The foreman even said that the county was going to pave the

road when they were through. That suited Kenny just fine. The washboard surface and mudholes of the dirt road made using his electric wheelchair on it a real chore.

Kenny sat on his porch now, staring across the road into the cornfield, thinking about all of this. The foreman had confirmed Kenny's fear that the waterline must be run underground (of course) to the back of the house where it could hook in with the existing pipes that ran up from the well pump. This could not be allowed to happen. The side lot contained his rose garden. His mama had planted it when his daddy was still alive—over twenty years ago. And with Mama gone that rose garden was his legacy, his memory of both of his parents. And over the years, he had used the beloved ground to bury the remains of the few strays that Mama had allowed him to keep and care for. Pets that he'd loved far more than he had ever loved any of the supposedly "real people" in his life. So the rose garden in the side yard was a memorial as well. Kenny would not sit idly by and see Mama's roses turned under, his memories exposed.

Even if he were physically capable, Kenny could not transfer the roses to the backyard. The ground was dark and rich in the side yard. It was easy to dig there. The backyard was littered with flat slabs of granite. The farmer who had built this house back in the 1930s had saved the large granite slabs when he cleared the surrounding land for farming. He had constructed a kind of rock patio back there. Nothing could grow there. The ground was impenetrable.

Kenny's house was essentially isolated on the road. To the left was a field of pole beans, to the right a plot of okra that gave way to watermelons and pumpkins at the fringes—all owned by

Daddy-Bob. Directly across the road from him was a thick field of corn. To the left of the corn was a cow pasture. To the right, the house that had those children who just about burned down the whole damn world the other day.

Kenny slitted his eyes and set his gaze straight ahead, just above the corn. All of his senses were wide open, seeing what he could draw to himself. To solve his dilemma. Kenny believed he had that power. Kenny believed he had many powers, but the key to it all was his ability to draw what he needed so that it came straight to him, so that the universe would deliver whatever it was that he needed right to his front door.

After a while, Kenny sensed a presence in the corn. A movement. From deep in the sticky green he heard a voice and set about drawing it to him.

KYLE WAS IN A FRENZY. HE WAS COMpletely lost in the field. The harder he tried to pinpoint the direction of Grace's voice, the more turned around he got. He would run in the direction he thought her voice was coming from, and when he got there and listened, she sounded farther away. He made himself stop. And listen. And wait for it. She hadn't called his name in what felt like a long time. Still, he forced himself to stand still, to set all his senses wide open, to see or smell or feel or hear anything that might lead him to Grace. A high-pitched scream broke the silence like shattering glass, but it was cut short. The scream was clipped like something bad had happened to the person doing the screaming.

It was enough for him to finally get a true sense of the direction. He took off to his left, running for all he was worth. He felt the rough corn fronds cut his cheeks. Kyle didn't care. And he didn't care about omens or retribution. He just knew that Grace needed to be saved.

Like entering a different world, Kyle broke through the corn into the bright sunlight of Eden Road. Directly in front of him, the paralyzed man was sitting on his front porch. And he had Grace.

His good arm was wrapped around Grace's head, so that the crook of his elbow covered Grace's mouth and face. Grace's Wonder Woman doll was gripped talon-like in his fat fingers. Grace in a million years would never voluntarily go up on the paralyzed man's porch. No kid would. So he knew right away that she'd been lured up there with that doll.

His good leg was hooked around Grace's thighs. His dead half just sat to the side, not moving. Grace was squirming like an impaled night crawler, but he had hooked her good. She wasn't going to get away from him on her own. She looked Kyle in the eyes and of course he saw the terror there, not the pretend terror from their games, but the true terror of having got herself into something more real than either of them had ever imagined.

Kyle stood in the middle of the road. He couldn't move. He reckoned he was in shock. He had never known an adult to snatch up a child that didn't belong to them. It just didn't happen. His daddy would shoot this man. If his daddy found out about this, he would shoot this man down dead. And nobody would ever say he did wrong.

"Boy, you've got work to do."

Kyle stood there mute.

"Do you understand? I know what you did. And I'll tell." His eyes cut to the doll in his fingers. "I've got the proof. Won't be no question about it."

And that's when Kyle finally realized what was behind all of this. The paralyzed man had them. He had the proof that they started that fire. That doll put them there. It proved that it was him and Grace that had burned down seventy-five acres of woods.

Kyle looked down between his feet and saw a dirt clod. It wasn't as good as a rock, but a dirt clod was hard like a rock. It was all that was there and Kyle wasn't thinking anyway. He was just reacting. Something deep inside of Kyle was telling him what to do, so he did it without thinking about it.

The dirt clod fit in his hand like it was custom made, and whatever was driving him had good aim. The hardened chunk of root bits and dried mud sailed through the air, and Kyle and the paralyzed man had time to hold each other's eyes, an understanding passing between them. Then the clod struck him straight on the forehead, right between the eyes. It exploded in a little puff of orange dust, leaving behind a thick, raised scum of dirt. Then the blood started flowing, washing the dirt away in a filthy little red trickle.

The paralyzed man let go of Grace and clapped his hand to the wound. Grace took off from the porch and crossed the road to Kyle. Kyle grabbed her hand and they took off like the devil himself was chasing them with his pitchfork.

And Kyle heard the paralyzed man's voice call out after them. And his voice was loud and clear, but it wasn't emotional or angry or anything like that. His voice was calm and certain. Sure of itself.

"Tonight, firebug. Be back here tonight. Midnight. Or I'll tell."

He WAS GETTING TO BE PRETTY GOOD AT acting normal when nothing in his life was normal at all. Mama fixed hot dogs and sauerkraut for dinner that night, and Kyle ate his fair share. After dinner, all of them went to the living room and watched Lawrence Welk on the TV. They ate vanilla ice cream with Hershey's Syrup while they watched it. Kyle stopped eating his ice cream for a minute and listened to the music of everybody's spoons clinking against their bowls while they ate their ice cream. It sounded good to him.

After that, Grace and Kyle had to go to bed since they were the youngest. Mama tucked them in, and she told Kyle he would not be going with his brothers to vacation Bible school next week. She said that they did not have enough money this year to sign him up for it. Kyle didn't care.

Later, in the dark, Grace asked him what was he going to do.

"I reckon I'll go on over there."

"No, Kyle, don't do it," she said.

"I reckon I have to. There ain't nothing else to do but to do it."

"That man grabbed hold of me."

"I seen it, didn't I?"

"Don't go."

"Grace, do you know what Daddy will do to us if he finds out we set that fire? Do you know? Do you have any kind of idea?"

They lay there in bed for a long time, listening to the others down the hall still up watching TV. Then, real quiet, Grace said, "Kyle?"

"What?"

"Will you get her back for me?"

"Your doll?"

She didn't say anything, but Kyle could feel the movement of Grace nodding her head in the dark.

"I reckon so," Kyle said.

JUST ABOUT A MONTH BEFORE KYLE ED-
wards lay awake in anticipation of his midnight meeting with
Kenny Ahearn, Sheriff's Deputy Officer Dana Turpin walked
down Eden Road, her department-issued shoes kicking up tiny
orange ground-level clouds in the July sun. It must have been
ninety-five degrees out there. Not a good day to pound the pave-
ment, or, in this case, the dirt.

Dana's black skin was so dark as to appear almost purple. She
would have liked to have lighter skin, and she was very much
aware of the fact that the brutal sun would turn her even darker.
She cursed herself for having left her cap in the patrol car. Vanity.
Pure vanity. She had given herself a relaxer at home the night
before and didn't want her uniform cap crimping her hair. Not
that it mattered, she thought. The humidity out here would puff
it up into an afro inside an hour.

Melodie Godwin's route from her home on Falls River Drive

to the Sweetwater Reservoir had only been three-and-a-half miles—assuming Melodie had taken the most direct route, and, at this point, there was no reason to assume otherwise. Melodie worked as a waitress at the Douglas Inn, and lived with her boyfriend in the house on Falls River Drive, just off of Lee Road. Dana didn't like the boyfriend, George Hicks, one bit. He had hands that looked like they wanted to hit. Something. Anything. Anybody. But he had been at his engine lathe at Anderson's Machine Shop all day except for a thirty-minute lunch that he had taken on-site in the break room. He was clear.

There was a party and cookout planned for noon at Sweetwater Reservoir—Melodie's niece was turning six. Melodie had called her mother from home to confirm the party at 10:30 that morning. She never showed up. No one had seen or heard from her since.

This was the second day of the investigation. Actually, it was the first day of the investigation, and the second day of the disappearance. Mrs. Godwin had reported her daughter missing a few hours after she failed to show up at the reservoir on Saturday, but Melodie was twenty-two years old, an adult, and adults were allowed to skip children's birthday parties without the sheriff's department hunting them down to find out why.

When Melodie failed to show up for her shift at the Douglas Inn Saturday evening and also did not return home that night, Mrs. Godwin called the sheriff's department every thirty minutes, certain that something was wrong. So, even though it had been less than the required twenty-four hours, the sergeant had gone ahead and assigned Dana to look into it. Just so they could tell the mother they were doing something. Normally, Dana was off on

Sundays, but she had dropped her daughter off at the babysitter's so she could get started. If harm had indeed come to Melodie Godwin, then every minute was critical. If Dana was going to take this as a serious matter, then starting the investigation could not be delayed. And in any event, she needed the extra hours.

Dana started with the basics. At seven that morning, she started knocking on doors. She wanted to talk with all of Melodie's neighbors. None of the neighbors appreciated being woken so early on a Sunday, but for the most part their irritation dissipated when Dana explained the reason for her intrusion. None of the neighbors had any information that Dana found useful. She drove the route between Falls River Drive and Sweetwater Reservoir three times (Melodie's mother having told Dana about the back road shortcut Melodie used to get there), but saw nothing that drew her interest. She visited the boyfriend (who was working from 6 AM until 2:30 PM that day, getting time and a half for a special order), but other than sensing a potential for violence just beneath his polite surface, Dana gleaned nothing of use for having interviewed him. Nothing.

A single phone call to her mother at 10:30 yesterday morning, then Melodie Godwin just disappeared completely.

After driving the short route for the third time, Dana got some lunch and then stopped by the station. She went into the file room where it was cool. She pulled a muscle in her shoulder reaching for a box of files looking for cases that involved Melodie's family members, boyfriend, or Melodie herself. Later, if necessary, Dana would look for records that involved Melodie's neighbors or coworkers. Dana found a single file, a domestic dispute between Melodie and her boyfriend. They had both been drunk, screaming, fighting loud. Neither had been arrested. Dana noted the name and address of the neighbor who had phoned in the complaint, and copied it in her notepad. She wondered why the neighbor had not volunteered the information this morning. It was clearly of importance.

When she followed up on it, the neighbor had not been home, so with no other ideas on how to proceed, Deputy Officer Dana Turpin decided to walk Melodie's assumed route that day. By now, it was going on three o'clock in the afternoon, the hottest part of the day. A three-and-a-half-mile hike in mid-July. Dana hitched her duty belt and started walking. The asphalt of Falls River Drive had absorbed so much of the sun's heat that the tarry surface was pliable, like black dough. Her dark blue uniform absorbed the brutal rays of sun, intensifying the heat. She could smell the raw polyester giving off fumes. The heat did ease the nagging pain from her shoulder, though. That was a nice bonus.

Dana scanned the environment as she walked up the residential road. She paid particular attention to the gutters and sewer grates. Just looking. Looking for anything.

FALLS RIVER DRIVE INTERSECTED WITH Lee Road. Lee Road was thick with churchgoers and truckers heading for I-20. The trucks roared past leaving her engulfed in back drafts of heavy, hot air that robbed Dana of her breath. But she was only on Lee Road for three-quarters of a mile before she came to Eden Road.

Eden Road began at a hidden juncture on Lee Road. A small stand of mimosa with outstretched, low-hanging limbs obscured the mouth of the road. And kudzu vines threatened to overtake the mimosa. An old-timey produce stand (*DADDY-BOB'S* it proclaimed, but Daddy-Bob was nowhere to be seen) stood there, otherwise there was nothing to mark it. No sign was erected. In fact, when driving the route, Dana had driven past it four full times before finally seeing it.

Dana figured that 99 percent of the people that drove past never noticed the road. And those that were aware of it used it only as a shortcut to the reservoir.

Instead of sewage grates, concrete gutters, and curbs, a rocky drainage ditch ran along both sides of Eden Road. Dana stopped often to toe through the accumulated debris or shift through the thick brambles. Looking. Just looking.

The road opened up and there was a pasture with a bull and grazing cows to her left, and a few houses to her right. The houses had generous space between them, and they were set well off the road. This was like a world unto itself. Like waking up on Walton's Mountain.

The scattered houses were mostly empty, this being Sunday. Church was an all-day affair for many folks: Sunday School, followed by a fire-and-brimstone service, ending with dutiful visits to the sick and infirm. Dana saw nothing out of the ordinary. She heard the pop of a .22 rifle, or maybe a firecracker, but couldn't locate the source. She saw a boy, still dressed in his Sunday suit, riding his bicycle down a long gravel driveway, and he had gone back to his house long before she made it to his driveway. That was the only house she had seen on the left side of the road. She studied it for a moment. It was nestled between the cornfield and a field of something Dana couldn't identify. The house looked safe.

Turning forward, something glinted in the drainage ditch. Dana went to investigate and plucked a tiny pebble of glass from the dirt. It was safety glass. The kind used in car windows that shatters into tiny pebble-like pieces instead of sharp shards like conventional glass. Dana used her pen and poked through the dirt looking for more. She found seven pieces of glass and put them in a small plastic bag. Probably nothing, Dana decided, but if it had been in the drainage ditch for very long, rain runoff would have worked it deeper into the earth or washed it away. She made a mental note to check to see if there had been any wrecks reported on this road.

She worked her way down the remainder of Eden Road. The stands of corn, pole beans, okra, peanuts, and potatoes gave way to dense woods that consisted mostly of scrub pine and pin oak. There was a horse paddock to the right, and Dana could see riding trails in the woods.

Eden road ended at Mt. Vernon Road, with the Sweetwater Reservoir directly across from it. Dana crossed the blacktop and was within twenty yards of the water. She rested a moment at the reservoir's edge. The duty belt with her weapon, ammunition, baton, two sets of cuffs, flashlight, police knife, and all the other paraphernalia she was expected to carry and trained to use, added at least eight pounds to her burden. And Dana was not a small woman. The breeze coming off the water refreshed her, but she was thirsty from the heat and all the sweating she had done.

Dana walked along the perimeter, passing by black men perched atop boulder-size hunks of Georgia granite scattered along the shore. The men fished using cane poles with bobbers weighted with lead sinkers and paid no attention to Deputy Turpin. It was peaceful down here, and Dana liked it.

A squat little cinder block building sat off to the right. The words *BAIT SHOP* had been spray painted on the side. Inside, it was shadowy and damp—not cool but humid and sticky. Dana saw earthworms, minnows, and crickets for sale. A sharp insect odor from the cricket cage burned in her nostrils.

Dana selected a bottle of Dr. Pepper from a pebbled aluminum chest cooler. The cooler hummed, and when she leaned over it she could feel warm air blowing up into her face from the wheezing compressor. Dana thought to herself that it was the bad compressor and the water from the open minnow tank that kept it hot and humid in here. The Dr. Pepper was ice-cold, though, and the glass bottle started sweating as soon as she pulled it out and popped off the metal cap with the bottle opener mounted with rusty pan screws to the cooler's side.

The old woman behind the counter was smoking a Kent. It dangled from her mouth, and she squinted against the smoke while she rang up Dana's drink.

"Mighty hot," Dana said to the old woman.

"Don't I know it."

"You work here most days?"

"Every day, I reckon," the woman said and took a long drag off her cigarette.

"Yesterday?"

The woman nodded, her expression communicating that she had just said as much.

Dana pulled a Polaroid photo from her uniform pocket. Melodie Godwin's mother had given it to her. In the photo, Melodie was smiling at something off camera. It was a bright, genuine smile, not the put-on smile people use for photographs. "Have you ever seen this girl? Yesterday maybe?"

The woman didn't take the Polaroid even though Dana was

holding it out, offering it to her. "Her mama's done been in here. She's a right pretty girl. I told her I ain't never seen her."

Dana took out her notepad and wrote her name and number on a piece of paper. "If she ever does show up, or you remember seeing her later, call me. Would you do that?"

"'Course I would. Right pretty girl. I hope nothing bad happened to her."

Dana sat on a concrete bench out-side the bait shop and drank her Dr. Pepper. It was delicious. Dana thought about the long, hot walk back to her patrol car on Falls River Drive. She was tempted to call her colleague, Senior Deputy Ben Hughes, to come down here and pick her up, but she knew doing that wouldn't get her any closer to finding Melodie. Deputy Turpin took out the Polaroid and studied Melodie's face. She really was pretty, and you could tell that whoever had taken the picture had really captured the essence of the girl. This made her think about Melodie's boyfriend and how his hands wanted to curl into fists. Dana pulled out the small plastic bag with the pieces of safety glass rolling around inside. She held the bag in one hand and the Polaroid in the other, as though comparing and contrasting them. She put them both away, stood up, stretched, noted no pain in her shoulder, and started walking back the way she had come.

GRANT JERKINS

* * *

ONCE SHE MADE IT PAST THE HORSE PAD-
dock, there were houses again. It was later now, and more folks
were back home from church. She showed the photo and asked her
questions, but nothing came of it—as she more or less expected.
But at least she was getting people to thinking about Melodie,
looking out for her.

From that direction, all of the houses were on the left side of
the road, with just one house on the right. It was the brick ranch
at the end of the long gravel driveway where she had seen the boy.
It was the house closest to where she had found the glass. When
she knocked, a woman came to the door. The woman was skinny
and looked pale and unhealthy with dark circles under her eyes.
She looked like someone who had recently lost a lot of weight.
Maybe to cancer. While the woman studied the photo, Dana
peered over the woman's shoulder into the house. The family was
still in their Sunday clothes eating dinner at a redwood picnic
table. Everyone at the table was looking up from their dinner,
looking at Dana to see what was going on. Except the father, he
kept his back to the door. There were three boys and a cute little
girl.

"No, ma'am, I'm sorry. I've never seen that girl," Louise Edwards said.

"I see you folks are eating supper, so I won't bother you anymore, but do you think you could tell me, do you ever remember
a car wreck up yonder above your driveway?"

"No. Never one that I can remember." Louise turned back to

the kitchen and said, "Boyd, do you ever remember anybody getting in a wreck up on the road?"

Boyd shook his head and stayed intent on his supper. Dana didn't like the way the man never turned around to look at her. Most men wouldn't let their wives answer the door to talk to the sheriff's department without getting themselves involved some kind of way. But it took all kinds. Dana also didn't like the look on the face of the youngest boy. As her daddy used to say, the boy looked as nervous as a whore in church. She made eye contact with him, but the boy looked away almost immediately. She saw fear in his eyes. Of course, lots of people were scared of the police. Especially kids. Didn't mean anything. Probably just like his daddy.

THE SUMMER DRAGGED ON, AND MELODIE
Godwin had disappeared without a trace. The case was officially
still open, but Dana's superiors had asked her not to devote any
more of her time into investigating it. There was no indication of
foul play, and the auto glass from the drainage ditch had no real
relevance. As her sergeant had put it, he could walk down the
street right now and find a handful of glass bits in the gutter. It
meant nothing. In light of the domestic disturbance call last year,
the assumption was that Melodie had gotten herself out of an
abusive relationship by simply disappearing. She got in her car,
started driving, and decided not to stop. Women did it every day.
Dana had argued that even if that were true, there was no reason
Melodie would fail to maintain contact with her mother or sisters.
The sergeant had said that she might be too embarrassed, then he
shrugged and said you just couldn't tell about some people.

But Dana still looked into it in her spare time, paying for day care or a sitter to watch her daughter. Mrs. Godwin called her almost every day. She felt that something bad had happened to her daughter, and no one would help her. Sometimes Mrs. Godwin would be waiting at the station house when Dana came in off her rotation. Dana could barely stand to look the woman in the eye.

So she tried. Whenever there was a spare moment, she would do something to nudge the case along. To try and push it just a little bit forward. Dana wanted to be able to look Mrs. Godwin in the eye and say she had done some little something to try and find her daughter. Sometimes she parked above George Hicks's house and just watched to see who came and who went, but nothing unusual ever happened. She still didn't like George Hicks, but her heart said the answer lay elsewhere.

She monitored Melodie's checking account for activity. There was none. This was usually considered a strong indication that the missing person had come to harm—a person can't survive without money. But Melodie only had forty-three dollars in her account. Not enough to bother with if she was simply fleeing an abusive relationship. And she had no credit cards.

Dana couldn't help but to keep coming back to Eden Road, and the boy who wouldn't meet her eyes. The other day, she had walked the road three times so that she could accidentally meet up with the boy. Even though she'd heard about the fire, she was still shocked when she saw that the side of the road that had held the vast expanse of woods and horse trails was a blackened blight. Burned to the ground. All the way to the reservoir.

On her third pass along the dirt road, Dana spotted movement on the porch of the house with the wheelchair ramp. She recognized the boy and decided to hang back and observe him for a moment. He was talking to a man in a wheelchair. It looked to Dana like the man was holding the boy's wrist, but she was too far away to be sure. She wished that she had brought her binoculars, but it had never crossed her mind that she might need them. The boy looked like he was trying to pull away from the older man, and Dana started moving forward. The sight had awakened something maternal in her. She didn't necessarily think the boy was in any kind of danger, but she felt that whatever was going on needed to be witnessed. The boy's sister emerged from the corn on the other side of the road and yelled something up to the porch. A few seconds later, the boy stumbled backward and fell on his rear end. He got to his feet, ran down the porch, and disappeared with his sister into the rows of corn.

By the time she made it to the house of the man in the wheelchair, the porch was empty, everything quiet. She studied the house. It was run-down with faded, peeling paint and shingles missing from the roof. Except for the wheelchair ramp, which stood out in sharp contrast with its newness. Dana turned and walked into the corn.

She tramped off through the stalks, but quickly realized that the rows were a kind of maze. The pun of *maze/maize* made her smile. All she could do was move forward and listen. After a while, the corn ended at the edge of a cow pasture. She caught sight of the boy and girl off to the left, moving across the sloping green field. Dana straddled the barbed wire fence and carefully maneuvered herself over it, but still managed to rip her pants at the inner thigh. She inspected the damage and saw that the barb had pierced her skin as well, though it didn't hurt. She made a mental note to check her personnel file for the date of her last tetanus shot—they were good for ten years.

Dana scanned the pasture but didn't see the boy and girl. There was a stand of weeping willows off to the right, so she headed in that direction. She circled around the stand and came at it from behind. She was able to approach without being seen. She could hear the children's voices. Her plan had been to walk right up and introduce herself and see if there was any way to gain the boy's trust, but she held back. The willow branches encircled the area like a green curtain, and Dana stood hidden in it, watching.

The boy was hanging upside down from a pendulous limb, swinging over a nasty-looking stagnant pond. He was trying to reach something in the green water, but it was just out of his grasp. The girl was pushing him so that he would swing out over the water. Dana smiled at the flag-colored cape the little girl was wearing. She recognized what it was immediately. Wonder Woman seemed to be everywhere that year. Along with Angie Dickinson as Sergeant "Pepper" Anderson and Lindsay Wagner as the Bionic Woman, powerful women were taking over television, and Dana watched all of those shows religiously. In fact, she had bought her daughter the same Wonder Woman costume from Zayre last Halloween. It wasn't really a Wonder Woman costume, but a cheap made-in-China "patriotic girl" outfit. Her daughter also had a doll version with the red calf-high boots, puffy black hair, and exaggerated bustline of the character as played by Lynda Carter.

Dana didn't think of herself as a women's libber, but she was only the fourth female sheriff's deputy officer in Douglas County, and the first black female deputy. She felt it every day. The stigma of being different. She made a conscious decision not to wallow in it, but she was certainly aware of it. It was there. So these silly little shows featuring women with superhuman strength, saving men, saving children, saving the day—they just delighted her. She knew that as important as it was for her to get out there and be visible, be competent, and not make mistakes, it was just as important the way these TV shows changed people's perceptions of women in general. She loved it. Now if they could just get some black folks on TV with a little more class than Sanford and Son.

The boy asked his sister to not push so hard and slow him down. It worked. Dana smiled when the boy plucked whatever it was that he was after from out of the water, but she realized even before the boy did, that he had gotten himself into a jam. He was stranded, upside down, over the water. The boy only had two options—up or down. Dana smiled again when the boy chose up and managed to right his body and began to scurry up the tapered branch like a monkey. She heard the leaves popping off the branch and saw the avalanche effect. The boy plunged into the water. It felt to Dana like he was down a long time. She had already taken two steps forward when the boy emerged, covered in green slime and algae.

The girl took off her play cape and gave it to the boy so that he could use it to wipe off the green slime. *That cape's ruined now*, Dana thought. Then the boy inspected what he had retrieved from the water. It was wrapped up in thread and it took a while to get it all unrolled. There was a silver dollar inside. The boy admired it for a while, and then he leaned over and hugged his sister. The boy turned away from her, and Dana could tell that he was crying. The girl started crying too.

Dana watched them a long time and knew that she would not speak to the boy on this day. She would not intrude. And it was only after she wiped the wetness from her cheek that Deputy Officer Dana Turpin realized that she had been crying too. And like Kyle and Grace, she didn't know why.

He DIDN'T HAVE ANY IDEA IF IT WAS MID-
night or not, so Kyle just laid there for a good long time after
everybody went to bed, and he could hear Mama and Daddy snoring. Grace had tried to stay up with him, but she was asleep too.
He crept out of bed and got himself dressed. It being a single level
ranch-style house, Kyle just opened the bedroom window and
crawled on out.

It was a long walk down the gravel driveway. Lonesome. There
were shrill insect sounds, and the skin on his arms looked funny
to him in the moonlight. There were odd sounds in the corn, and
Kyle thought that he could hear someone moving around in
there. That got him to thinking about Soap Sally. Mama said that
when Soap Sally grabbed little kids, those needle-fingers would
poke them over and over again like getting a thousand shots at the
doctor's office. He started walking a little bit faster. When he got
to the road, he could see a dim light seeping through the paralyzed

man's front window. To Kyle, the light looked greenish, like a witch-light.

There wasn't anything to do but walk up the ramp and knock on his door. Kyle could never in a million years imagine a future for himself that included him knocking on the front door of the paralyzed man at midnight. Never.

Because of the wheelchair and him being dead on one side, the paralyzed man kind of sidled up to the door so he could still reach it but not block it with his chair. He smiled at Kyle real big with those yellow teeth with the black rot spots.

"Boy, I didn't think you'd really come."

When Kyle got inside, the green light wasn't like a witch-light at all. One of the lights had a green shade was all. It was actually kind of nice. It made him feel warm inside like a good fire in the wintertime. The door shut behind him.

"What's your name, boy?"

"Kyle, sir."

"Kyle. That's a fine sheet. You're a fine boy. Scared?" Kyle assumed the man meant "name" when he said "sheet."

"No, sir."

"Why not? I'd be scared."

Kyle just shrugged.

"You a firebug, Kyle?"

"No, sir."

"Coulda fooled me. Boy burns down damn near a hundert acres of timber, I'd say that boy was a firebug."

"Can I have the doll back?"

The paralyzed man seemed to give the question a great deal

of thought. Finally, he nodded and said, "'Course you can. I don't aim to punish you. That's The Lord's work. Thy will be washing machine."

Done! Kyle wanted to scream at him, completely unnerved by what he did not realize was the paralyzed man's extremely mild case of Wernicke's aphasia brought on by the stroke. *Thy will be done!*

The paralyzed man dug down under his lap and pulled out Wonder Woman, her metal wristbands glinting. He held her out to Kyle, and when Kyle reached out, he pulled the doll back. Kyle felt the doll's black nylon hair tickle his skin. "We just got a little work to do first. The shovel's in the shed out back yonder."

KYLE WAS SCARED OUT THERE BECAUSE of the way the pole beans were planted—nobody could see him if something were to happen. The task seemed simple enough, though. The man wanted his rosebushes dug up out of the side yard and moved to the other side before the county crew tore through them to run the waterline. It was actually quick work. The ground was soft, loamy, and the roses' roots were somewhat shallow. He was wearing thick gloves to protect him from the thorns. First he dug good wide receiving holes on the far side of the yard, then he dug up the rosebushes one at a time and moved them to the new holes before the roots could dry out. The paralyzed man watched him from the porch, telling him how to do it, that green light leaking out from behind him. Why this had to be done at midnight, Kyle didn't know.

Once the last bush had been set back in the ground, he sent Kyle back to the side yard where he had excavated all the bushes.

"Roots, boy. Run deeper than you think. You don't get them out, why the bush'll ceiling fan right back up."

Sprout, Kyle thought. *The bush'll sprout right back up.*

"Wouldn't that be a good thing? Then you'd have roses on both sides of your house."

"No. They graft. In the nursery, they graft fine roses, like those Mr. Lincolns you just dug up. They graft them onto rootstock. Substandard rootstock. Ain't no telling what might sprout up. It's best to get it all out. Kill it."

Kyle sighed and started digging again. He was tired and wanted to go home. Kyle just wanted the paralyzed man to give him that doll and let him go home and forget all about him and the roses and the fire.

"Deeper, dig a little deeper, son."

It didn't make sense. If there weren't any roots right here, how could there be more roots farther underground?

"Deeper," he said. His voice was soft and high. "Don't want it haunting me next spring. Keep digging."

Kyle figured he was right, because pretty soon he hit a hard root system. He chopped at it with the shovel blade to loosen it up, but it was tight, knotted up. Thick. He set the shovel blade over it and jumped up and down on the back of the shovel until he heard and felt the root snap. Kyle reached down and yanked at it. It came up easy enough, a big clot of root shaped like a hand. It felt funny to him. Soft and rotted. And he smelled it. Kyle threw it down because he realized it wasn't a root at all. It really was a hand. A creaky little scream came out of his mouth, like a ten-penny nail being pulled from damp lumber.

It was somebody's hand. He was digging up a body.

The paralyzed man was framed in the front door, sitting high up on that metal chair, the green light spilling out all around him. Kyle could see now that it really was witch-light. And the paralyzed man was laughing. Laughing to beat the devil.

THE SPACES IN THE WEB WERE FILLING

in now.

She remembered who she was. *Melodie.* Her name was Melodie Godwin. She remembered how she got here. She had been running late for the party. The party! Her mother, her sisters, her nieces and nephews. What she would give to be with them right now. Normalcy. There had been a boy on a bicycle. A stupid boy. A stupid, stupid boy. Coming around a blind curve in the middle of the road. Yes, she had maybe been going faster than she should have. She'd nearly killed him. It was nothing more than the grace of God that she had been able to swerve at the last possible second. The car had ended up on its side in a ditch. She remembered that her head had been bleeding, her fingernails somehow torn off. And she remembered finding a metal wrench that George had left in there, and using it to break out the passenger window. She had climbed out of the car and asked the boy to help her. And the boy—the stupid, stupid boy—had run away from her.

Then the monster had appeared. The monster was wearing a disguise that made him look like a harmless old man. Bald head with wisps of fine white hair. Pudgy and soft-looking. Christian. He said he was Christian.

He had a tow truck. And he pushed the car, got it rocking, until it landed on its tires back in the road. The monster towed her car to his house—the next house up the street. He took Melodie into his house and lay her down on the living room couch. He'd even put a cool dishrag on her head. She had gone to sleep then. A black sleep from the head wound.

The monster was strong. His disguise made him look weak. But when Melodie woke up, he was carrying her. She remembered that quite clearly, but it was a single sensation of being cradled and the image of the monster's smiling disguise looking down at her.

Then she stayed in the dark. Her leg was chained, and she could move in a small circle around the metal pole she was chained to. He came to her in the dark. He did hateful things to her in the dark. Hurtful, hateful things. He had stuck a needle into her throat. He injected something into her throat. It burned and it burned and it burned. She could feel it like acid eating away at her. And when the burning had gone away, she could not talk. She could not scream, she could not whimper—she was no longer able to make any sounds at all. The monster stuck other things inside her.

He brought her smelly table scraps to eat. Sometimes the food was spoiled and had thick, fuzzy mold growing on it. One time when she reached in the dark to scoop the scraps from the bowl that was bolted to the floor, she had scooped up a mouse. It scurried through her fingers with a little *eek* and ran away. And then after just a few days, the monster had stopped coming to her. He stopped bringing her the table scraps. And the little bowl of water she lapped from went dry. Now the mouse was hungry too. She could sometimes hear the soft scratch of its tiny claws searching for scraps in the empty metal bowl.

Melodie came to believe that the monster was dead. And her mind started to fill back in. Where before she had existed on the most primitive level of her brain, just a skeletal web of function and survival, when the monster stopped coming, she allowed her mind to fill in again. She allowed herself to remember that she was Melodie Godwin, and she allowed herself to remember what the monster had done to Melodie Godwin.

And the seam. She had found the seam. Just a rough edge of what felt like plastic at the apogee of her reach. She could just flick it with the tips of her injured fingers. During every period of wakefulness, Melodie worked at stretching and lengthening her cords, joints, and tendons. Every tiny increment of length helped, until the time came when she could play her fingers lightly over the seam, but couldn't quite get them under it so that she could pull on it. While she worked at it, Melodie thought of the old Lee Dorsey song, *Working in the Coal Mine*. She would have liked to hum it while she worked, but, of course, her vocal cords had been dissolved with a hypodermic shot of Drano. (He'd told her on the second day that it had been Drano. "Just a drop. A dab'll do ya," he'd said, and if she wasn't good, she'd "get a shot of it up her twat.")

After a long while, her strength had dissipated. She had had no food or water in a very long time. A week, at least. She decided to catch the mouse and eat it. She had never bothered the mouse before, so it was not leery of her, and it accepted her presence as normal. She knew that she would only have one chance; for once she made her intentions known, once she became a predator, the rodent would go nowhere near her. So, in the dark, she waited and listened. Even though she had licked it clean long ago, Melodie licked the inside of the bowl, hoping her saliva might activate a dormant food smell. She held her hand well above the empty bowl, poised to strike, so that she would be ready when the time came. It was excruciating to hold her arm out like this for so long a time. After what felt like hours of holding her arm raised and ready to strike, it went numb, so she was unsure if her aim would be true when the time came. And that time came at long last. She heard the soft scratching of the tiny paws, searching for microscopic bits of food. Melodie did not hesitate. She brought her hand down in a deathblow.

There was no repulsion, no talking herself into doing it. She tore off the rodent's head with her teeth and drank the blood greedily. As good as the flesh had tasted, as delicious as the sensation of actually *chewing* something had been—she was dehydrated more than anything else.

She sucked the bones for a long time, enjoying the smooth feel of them in her mouth. And then she realized, the bones were *tools*. She selected a curved rib bone, and stretched herself out to the seam. She was able to get the arched bone under the seam with no problem. It slid under the seam as though it were a specialty tool constructed for that purpose alone. She rolled the bone and she heard and sensed the seam pop up. In fact, she saw it. A faint glow. With the edge of the seam popped up, the plastic stuck out enough for her to grasp it between thumb and forefinger. She pulled, and more of it came free. There was daylight far behind the seam. A razor thin beam fell across the wood floor. She adjusted her grip, clenching the black plastic in her hand, and pulled with all her strength.

Light flooded her world. Painful, painful light. It was a window. Once her eyes had adjusted to the new presence of light, she saw that she was in an attic, and that the walls and even the ceiling had been covered in thick layers of black plastic garbage bags secured with duct tape.

By standing at the very limits of her chain, she could see out the window. She could see a dirt road. The dirt road. Eden Road. And beyond the road, she could see a field of corn bordered by a pasture dotted with cows. And farther off, what looked like a boy and a girl. And a green pond.

It was just starting to get light outside when he crawled back through the window. Grace was asleep, and Kyle saw that she was sucking her thumb and clutching a pillow since she didn't have her Wonder Woman doll to hold on to.

Kyle didn't want to get in the bed with her. He smelled like death. He'd washed himself with the garden hose, but the smell from those bodies still hung on him. The paralyzed man had brought out a flashlight to make sure Kyle got all the pieces. Some of it was just like a skeleton in the movies, but some of it was wet and runny. It wasn't hardly human. Kyle reckoned he must have cut them up into pieces before he buried them out there. It ended up taking four garbage bags before it was all cleaned up.

He crawled on in the bed with Grace, bringing that smell of death with him. There wasn't nothing else to do.

THE THROBBING IN HIS GOOD WRIST
wouldn't stop. He had fallen down the stairs. Stupid. The stupid
nurse must have measured the shot wrong. (*I'm not a nurse, Mr.
Ahearn, I'm a health care assistant*, she'd always say. Whatever.) She
fixed him up a week's worth and laid them out on a dish towel in
the Frigidaire. But she must have measured wrong. His sugar had
dropped and he'd gotten dizzy and fell.

If the wrist was broken, Kenny would be essentially incapaci-
tated. He was slowly regaining use of his paralyzed side. In fact,
the nurse—excuse me, health care assistant—wouldn't be coming
back. Said the Medicaid wouldn't cover it anymore.

He had been able to get up and down stairs for some time now,
so instead of sleeping on the couch in the living room, he could
go upstairs to sleep in his own bedroom, or up to the attic if he
was feeling frisky. The nurse had taught him how. Kenny would
put a crutch under his right arm, and hold on to the handrail with
his good left. The good left leg would go up the step first—while

keeping his weight on the crutch and the handrail. Then he would just sort of drag the right side of his body—crutch and all—up to the same step. He reversed the process to come back down. It took a damn long time. But it worked. Except this morning he had a sugar spell and had fallen from the third step. His wrist was sprained (hopefully not broken), but otherwise he was fine.

The boy was young and strong; let him do the work. He was in it with the boy now. They had each other.

Kenny used his mind to draw the boy to him. He set the thoughts in motion and waited for the universe to deliver.

He knew it had been a big risk, using the boy to clean up his mess. The boy could be home right now, telling his parents. The police might be on their way this very minute. But what choice did he have? The county workers would have found his discarded pets. What a God Almighty mess that would have been. Body parts strewn across the yard.

There was a knock at the kitchen door. Kenny peeked out the front window and saw a green Pontiac Catalina sitting in the driveway. Opal Phillips! *For the love of God.* He went to the door and smiled warmly at Opal. She was holding a Pyrex casserole dish nestled in a little yarn cozy she had undoubtedly crocheted herself. *Christ, give me strength.* Kenny reversed his chair and ushered Opal into the kitchen. She leaned over and kissed him on the forehead, and Kenny could just feel the lipstick staining his head like malignant melanoma.

"Oh, Kenny, how are you getting along?"

Already she was starting in on the longing looks. Kenny could feel his skin crawl. This was not what he had asked the universe to deliver.

"Fine. Just fine. You are so good to come see me, Opal."

"Why Kenny, I just think about you nearly every day. You need a woman around here to look out for you."

"You are too sweet," Kenny managed, his mouth already dry as lint.

"Just look at your face. It's a mess." Opal produced a Kleenex seemingly from nowhere, and swooped down on Kenny. She picked away the tight little balls of white spit that had formed at the corners of his mouth. God, how he hated her.

"Opal?"

"What is it, dear?"

"I need to tell you something."

"Go right ahead."

"I've developed feelings. About you. Feelings about you."

A fire lit in her eyes. "Feelings?"

"Yes, and I need time. Time to pray on it. Time to sort out what I'm feeling. To talk to God."

"Why Kenny you don't have—"

"I'm on a spiritual journey now. Spiritual."

"But God wants us to—"

"None of us knows what God wants."

"But, Kenny, I care for you too. You know that."

"I need guidance. From The Lord."

"Of course. We all do."

"And time. To pray. I just ask you that. You better go."

Confusion replaced—but didn't extinguish—the fire in Opal Phillips's eyes. She wasn't sure what had just happened. Was it victory? Or defeat? It was hope, she decided.

"Kenny Ahearn, you talk to God. And I will too."

"I want you to stay away for a while. I think it's best."

"You'll call me? When you're ready?"

"I'll call. But give me time."

LATER, KENNY SAT ON HIS PORCH. HE WAS changing. It wasn't like him to toy with Opal like that. What was wrong with him? Maybe it was the stroke. He indulged in a day-dream imagining that he had indeed been caught, that the county crew had unearthed the bodies. He imagined how the sight would have sickened them. The police would be called. Newspaper reporters would show up, shouting Kenny's name, hoping for a quote. The Atlanta TV stations might come down here too. The church people would be shocked to their very souls, and they would tell the TV reporters that Kenny Ahearn was a quiet man, a good Christian man. And Opal. Opal Phillips would be shaken to her crocheted core. Kenny giggled.

Across the road, the corn parted and the boy emerged. The universe had delivered. Kenny flipped a switch on his wheelchair, and the motor hummed low as he navigated it into the house. The boy followed.

THEY SAT THERE AT HIS KITCHEN TABLE. IT was like they were friends and he was having Kyle over for a glass of milk. Except they had been sitting there at the table, not saying anything, for a good long while. And it wasn't milk in the tall glass sitting in the middle of the table. No, the fluid in the glass was a cool neon blue. It could've been Kool-Aid, maybe. But it wasn't that either. Kyle knew what it was. It was Liquid Drano. The tall red, white, and blue bottle it came out of was sitting right next to the glass. He had made Kyle pour it, because he said his wrist was sprained. Tough on clogs, the bottle proclaimed. Won't hurt pipes.

The paralyzed man's eyes were blue too, like the sky might look over the North Pole. They were so blue that they hurt Kyle. They cut him. And he could feel it all over, those eyes cutting into him, trying to get into his mind. Trying to charm him.

"I can make you drink that," he said. "Do you believe me?"

Kyle didn't answer him, because he did believe him. Kyle did believe that he could make him drink it. That he would end up just like Joel Sewell. He would be disfigured. He could imagine the way it would feel in his mouth, how it would burn away his tongue and eat his flesh.

"Now I don't mean that I'll physically force you to do it," the paralyzed man said, and Kyle noticed that he didn't mix up his words anymore like he used to. Like he was getting better. "I mean that if I tell you to, you will pick up that glass of acid and drink it."

He just stared at Kyle and held him in those polar eyes, cutting him up like a thousand frozen knives.

"Pick it up."

Kyle didn't move.

"Your sister will do whatever I say. I can call her over here. With my mind. Do you believe that? I changed her. I put a piece of me inside her. Do you want me to summon her now? She'll drink it for me."

The thought of the paralyzed man putting Grace under his spell was all it took. The thought of him tricking her into tasting the pretty blue drink. Kyle reached out. The glass was warm, like the acid was giving off heat. Kyle picked it up. He couldn't resist those eyes. He couldn't. He couldn't. He couldn't. He couldn't. He couldn't.

He couldn't.

Kyle took the thick fluid into his mouth.

It coated his tongue, and he spit it right back out. He waited for the pain, for the burning. But it didn't come. The paralyzed man was laughing. He was laughing so hard his face turned red and tears came out the corner of his eyes. He reached out with his sprained hand and gingerly picked up the metal Drano bottle. He took a deep chug off it. "It's cornstarch and unsweetened Kool-Aid, boy. I wouldn't kill you. Not yet. Do you think I'm crazy? You've got work to do. Now listen, I want you to reach up in that cabinet there and reach down them crackers." Kyle got up and did like he told him. "Them orange ones right there," he said. "Now reach in the Frigidaire there and get a co-cola. Now run that upstairs. To the attic. My pet's hungry."

"In the attic?"

"Yes, boy, the attic. She's a mouser. Catches 'em and eats 'em."

"And you want to feed her crackers and co-cola?"

"You ever ate a mouse? Ain't very filling. Now you run along and be back directly. Directly, you hear?"

And then she could tell day from night. With the window exposed, she felt the passage of time. She enjoyed the daylight and the view of the outside world, but she was starving to death. Her lips were hard and dry like crinkled tinfoil, and she had no saliva in her mouth with which to lick them.

And then one day she heard people outside the house. Men working with nails and hammers and electric saws. Their voices, muffled, floated up to her. She had no way to signal them. Nothing to throw at the window. She had no voice with which to scream. She could perhaps try banging on the floor with her fists or her heels, but she had no strength. She could no longer move. She was dying.

The next day, the monster came back. When she heard the cars pull up the drive, Melodie found the strength to stand up and look out the window. She saw a station wagon and an old Ford pickup. Two men hopped out of the pickup's cab and set about unloading a heavy-looking wheelchair from the bed. A woman dressed like a nurse opened the back door of the station wagon. The monster was inside. The woman dressed like a nurse reached in the car and pulled the monster up to her. She held him braced against her hip, pivoted, and dropped him expertly into the seat of the waiting wheelchair. The monster tried out his wheelchair. His disguise was grinning. He drove the chair out of sight, then back into the driveway. Each of the men clapped the monster on the shoulder, then climbed back into the pickup and drove away. The nurse and the monster came into the house.

Later, after the nurse left, Melodie thought that the monster would come for her, but he did not. Days passed. The attic held all of the heat from the house as it baked in the midsummer sun, but Melodie could no longer sweat as her body was so dehydrated. Her skin looked wrinkled, mummified.

On the third day after his return, Melodie heard the monster on the stairs. There was the creaking door. Then the familiar sharp hollow sound of a boot striking a wooden step. That was followed by a new sound: a little rubber squeak. And then the rustling sound of the monster dragging its dead part up the step. And again. The hollow strike, the tiny squeak, the dragging of the dead part. And again.

The attic door opened and Melodie's first thought was that the monster had changed his disguise from harmless old man to some kind of robot. His head was covered in a metal helmet and long lenses of steel and glass protruded from his eyes. And then Melodie recognized that he was wearing night vision goggles. Her daddy had brought a pair just like them back from Korea. And she understood that was how the monster was able to see her and do those things to her in the blackout room.

"Still alive? Just barely, I see." The monster unbuckled the strap under his chin and the goggles fell to the floor. He pivoted on his crutch and reached down into his pocket. He tossed a can of Coca-Cola and a package of fluorescent orange Toast Chee crackers at her. He leaned against the wall and looked around the room, nodded at the little pile of mouse bones, then lifted the cane to indicate the exposed window with remnants of black plastic hanging from it. "You've got it looking right pretty in here."

He watched Melodie fumble with the can of Coca-Cola. Even if she had fingernails to pry up the pull-ring, she clearly didn't have the strength. "Reach it back up to me." The monster wedged the can between his body and the crutch, removed the pull-ring, and dropped it on the floor. "Scooch back." Melodie complied, and the monster poured the soda into the bowl, the precious dark liquid sloshing and fizzing and spilling over the rim onto the wood plank floor. Melodie rolled onto her stomach and lapped from the bowl. The effect to her body was like a shot of amphetamine—an instantaneous jolt. When she looked up, the paralyzed man was already gone. She realized now that he wasn't a monster at all. He was just a man, paralyzed and broken.

A monster could not be beaten, but a man could.

Melodie used her teeth to tear open the package of crackers. The smell hit her like an electric current. She devoured one, then two, then three. She decided to save the remaining three crackers, to ration them, but then she ate a fourth one. Then she ate the fifth. The last cracker she wrapped back up in the cellophane package and saved it for thirty minutes before she went back to it and ate it and licked the cellophane clean. Melodie saved the wrapper;

hid it out of sight under one of the black plastic trash bags that she had torn from the window.

Off to the side, just within her range of reach, Melodie spotted the pull-ring from the can of Coca-Cola on the floor where the paralyzed man had dropped it. She retrieved it and hid it under the plastic bag too. The night vision goggles were beyond her reach.

It turned out that there was no reason to ration the crackers, because the paralyzed man returned once a day. He always brought the same thing—a can of Coke and a pack of peanut butter crackers. He said it was all he could fit in his pockets. She could tell that the paralyzed man was getting stronger. It took him less and less time to get up the stairs, and his speech was growing clearer. And he was looking at her again, in that way. And Melodie understood that before long the hurting would start again. But she was growing stronger as well. And every day he dropped the pull-ring on the floor, and every day, Melodie retrieved it. She had ten now. She discovered that she could crimp the metal ring around the end of her finger so that it held tight, and the curved metal tab would extend from her fingertip in a sharp claw. The metal was weak and flimsy, but the edges were sharp. With a set of ten, she would have opportunity for one good cutting swipe before they broke or bent. If she got his eyes, once would be enough.

Melodie heard the familiar strike/squeak/rustle sound on the step. She was ready. She was wearing her pull-ring claws. She held her hands out to look at her creation one last time. To her, her hands looked like an Indian goddess. She didn't know which one, but she remembered seeing a picture in a book of a Hindu woman with elongated metal fingertips.

The aluminum rings were cutting into her skin where she had crimped them tight, but they had to be good and secure if she was going to use them as a weapon. The oval tabs curled out and under, like talons. She could do some real damage. She put her hands behind her back and waited. But something happened. She heard the sound of the boot strike and squeak countered with the dragging of the dead part only twice more. Then there was faint muffled noise. Then nothing. The paralyzed man never came.

She waited a long, long time. Hours it seemed. She was ready to do this now. She had about given up and was going to take off her metal claws when she heard footsteps on the stairs. They were light, and made soft little squeaks instead of heavy strikes. Whatever it was (maybe the monster had a helper), something was coming up. Melodie hid her hands behind her back and relished the musical sound of her metal talons clicking together.

KYLE OPENED THE DOOR AT THE TOP OF
the stairs.

His mouth was still slimy from the cornstarch. He felt like he
was a zombie. He had seen a movie on channel 17 called *White
Zombie* with Bela Lugosi. A man and a woman go down to Haiti
and down there a shaman can bring back the dead. Once you're
brought back from the dead, you can't think for yourself anymore, and you're under the control of the one that brought you
back. That's how he felt. Like he wasn't thinking for himself anymore. The paralyzed man had him under his control. It was easier
to be under someone else's control, to not have to think for yourself. If he was thinking for himself, he sure as hell would not have
knowingly taken a swallow of Drano, not knowing full well what
it had done to Joel. And if the paralyzed man could control Joel

like that, then why wouldn't he be able to make Kyle do any damn thing he pleased?

Kyle was lost.

He smelled that something was very wrong before he even opened the door. He figured the cat must have died up here. It smelled foul—like feces and urine and blood and sour sweat. Inside the attic was covered from floor to ceiling with black plastic. There was a pole in the middle. And there was a naked woman chained by one ankle to the pole. Kyle knew right away it was Soap Sally. She looked just like he imagined Soap Sally would look like. Wild, her eyes vacant. No soul. Then he saw this woman was young, way too young to be Soap Sally. It was the woman from the wrecked car. She was alive. When Kyle looked in her eyes, he saw that she wasn't really seeing him at all.

Her hair was matted up real bad, and there was blood caked and dried on her legs. Kyle dropped to his knees and sat down the soda pop and crackers. "Ma'am? Are you alright?" She opened her mouth to talk, but the only sound that came out was a coarse grunt—air mostly. Kyle saw that something was wrong with her throat. She had some bubbles of wet-looking scar tissue around her neck. It reminded him of Joel, but not nearly as bad. "Ma'am, are you hungry?" He pushed the food toward her, and when he did her hands came out from behind her back and she jumped at him. They weren't needles like Soap Sally, but the woman had metal claws on her fingertips. She slashed him across the face with them, and Kyle was marked. He felt blood pool up on his cheek, under his eye. She reared back to swipe him again, and he lunged backward. She came right after him, and she would have had him easy except the chain around her ankle stopped her cold. She lay on the floor, flailing and swiping in the air with those metal talons.

Kyle ran. He fell down the stairs, and picked himself up at the bottom. The paralyzed man was watching him from the kitchen, and when Kyle stood up, he started laughing. Kyle ran past him and out the door. He could still hear him laughing.

Mᴀᴍᴀ ᴡᴀɴᴛᴇᴅ ᴛᴏ ᴋɴᴏᴡ ᴡʜᴀᴛ ʜᴀᴅ ʜᴀᴘ-
pened to his face. Kyle told her that Mr. Ahearn was paying him
to help him around his house, and that Kyle was digging up his
rosebushes for him. Kyle said the thorns had got him. She went
to the bathroom and came back with the Mercurochrome. The
smell of it stung his nose just as soon as she had the cap off it. She
blew a stream of cool air over the cuts, then tilted his head back
so that his face was in good light and she started to daub it on.
Kyle braced himself against the pain, but it never came. Not to say
that it didn't hurt, because it did. It burned and stung like a hundred yellow jackets, but for some reason the pain was just another
part of him, neither bad nor good, just there. Maybe being a zombie wasn't all bad.

She kissed him on the forehead and said he was a good boy to
help out Mr. Ahearn, but Kyle didn't think she thought twice
about it, about whether it was okay for a ten-year-old boy to spend
his time alone with a grown man—even if he was in a wheelchair.

DANA TURPIN FOUND THE BOY BACK AT the green pond. He was alone this time. She wanted to talk to him. The way he had looked away from her that Sunday afternoon still bothered her. She just needed to talk to him and satisfy herself that nothing was there.

She had parked her car at a high spot along Eden Road. It gave her a good view of everything that went on. It was mostly quiet. About ten in the morning she saw the older brothers head off toward the reservoir through the scorched void that used to be woods. A little while after that, she saw the youngest boy emerge from the house by himself. He disappeared into the corn. About five minutes later, he emerged from the corn directly onto Eden Road. If he had looked to his right, he would have seen Dana sitting in her little green Chevette. Since she was off duty, she didn't have her patrol car, of which she was glad, because she knew the sight of a patrol car would likely have spooked the boy. But he never saw her. He stepped into the road and crossed it without ever looking either way. *Good way to get yourself killed*, Dana thought, and hoped her own daughter would have more sense than that. The boy crossed into the yard of the house directly across the street. It was the house with the ramp and the green-shingled roof. The boy walked up the wheelchair ramp, onto the front porch, and entered the house without knocking.

Dana knew that the house belonged to Kenny Ahearn. That Mr. Ahearn was a church deacon who had recently had a stroke. But she had yet to talk to him directly. He had been back from the hospital a good while now, so she should go by and talk with him, but from what she had learned indirectly, he seemed like a good man. The kind of man who would step forward and volunteer information if he had any. She figured the boy must be doing some chores for Mr. Ahearn. (And Dana knew full well that the boy's name was Kyle Edwards, but for some reason, when she thought of him, she thought of him as "the boy.")

About thirty minutes had passed when Dana heard the front door bang open and looked up to see the boy jump off the porch and race across the road into the cornfield. She could see the tops of the cornstalks moving and could tell that he was going back to his house.

About forty-five minutes after that, he came back out again. And again, he crossed through the cornfield, but this time he emerged on the far side where the field bordered the cow pasture. Dana got out of her car and followed him.

She was more careful crossing over the barbed wire fence this time, and as she approached the dense weeping willows that surrounded the pond, she cleared her throat to announce her presence and not startle the boy.

He was throwing rocks into the pond, but stopped and looked at Dana as she emerged through the hanging branches. The first thing she noticed was the stark change in the boy. His complexion was an unhealthy yellow, and the skin under his eyes was darkly bruised. The boy looked haunted.

"Hey, how you doing?"

"Fine, I reckon."

"You remember me?"

"Sure. You're the police lady that was looking for that woman."

"You've got a pretty good memory. What's your name?"

"Kyle. Kyle Edwards."

"I'm Dana. Dana Turpin. Pleased to meet you." Kyle met her extended hand with his own, and Dana noted that the boy's flesh was cool and damp. Dana motioned to the boy's face. "How'd you cut yourself?"

The boy touched the fresh cuts lightly with his fingertips, as if just now remembering they were there. "Oh, that was nothing. I was digging up some rosebushes and got cut on the thorns."

"You've got to be careful." Dana studied the boy a moment longer, not liking what she was seeing. "Her name is Melodie," Dana said. "The woman who went missing, her name is Melodie Godwin." Kyle went back to throwing rocks in the pond. "Her folks are mighty worried. They still hope she might show back up."

"Maybe she will," Kyle said.

"You don't know anything about it, do you Kyle?"

Kyle threw two more rocks into the green pond before he answered. "No, ma'am, I sure don't."

Dana nodded and said, "'Cause, if you did, you would need to tell me so that I can find her and her mama can stop worrying.

Can you imagine what her mama must be feeling?" Dana pulled the Polaroid of Melodie out of her pocket and handed it to Kyle. "This is what she looks like." Kyle studied the picture for a long time before handing it back.

"I sure am sorry she got hurt."

"Hurt? Do you think she got hurt?"

"Well I just reckon something bad must of happened to her."

"Kyle, do you ever remember any car getting in a wreck on Eden Road?"

"I don't know."

"You don't know?"

"No, ma'am."

"I want to show you something, Kyle." She handed Kyle the plastic evidence bag that she still carried with her like a memento. Or a charm. "That's auto glass. I found it in the ditch right up from the end of your driveway. Somebody banged up their car. I thought there was a good chance you might have seen it."

Kyle stood up and brushed off the backside of his jeans. "I have to get on back home. My mama will be worried."

"I understand. I want to give you something, Kyle." Dana reached into her pocket for her pen and notepad, wrote, and tore off the sheet. "This is my name and my telephone number. I want you to promise to call me if you remember anything. Will you promise me that, Kyle?"

Kyle pocketed the paper, said, "Yes, ma'am. I promise," and ducked his way through the willow branches.

Dana scooped up a handful of pebbles and began tossing them into the green pond. The scummy surface was so clogged with algae that the water didn't even ripple. Kyle knew something. She was certain that Kyle was concealing something. And as certain as she was that Kyle would be the key to finding out at least something about Melodie, she was equally certain that if she pushed him, that key would be lost. He was a fearful child, a haunted child. Something was eating at Kyle's conscience. Kyle would have to come around on his own. Dana would try to think of subtle ways to get him moving in the right direction, but if she pushed too hard, the fear would overtake him and Kyle would shut down.

Dana stood and brushed off the seat of her pants just as Kyle had done, and she realized that in her thoughts, during that brief exchange, he had gone from being "the boy" to being "Kyle."

KENNY SMILED UP AT THE COLORED PO-
licewhore and said, "Yes, ma'am, that's me, Kenny Ahearn. It's
awful hot today, why don't you sit and rest yourself a minute?"

"I thank you," the colored policewhore said and sat her fat
black ass in the porch swing. "I thank you very much." Kenny
could tell that she was purposefully adding a little Southern twang
to her voice, trying to put him at ease: *We're all just folks here.*

"Now what can a man like me do to help Douglas County's
finest?"

"Well, sir, first off, I'm Deputy—"

"Ma'am," Kenny interrupted. "Can I get you something to
drink? Would you like a nice ice-cold glass of Kool-Aid?"

"No, sir, thank you anyway."

"Well what about a nice cold slice of watermelon? Got some
in the Frigidaire right this minute."

"No. Thank you all the same."

She'd dropped the twang, Kenny noted with satisfaction. He'd put that bitch on notice.

"As I was saying, I'm Deputy Officer Turpin. Dana Turpin, and I've been trying to get by to talk to you for quite a while now. You're a hard—"

"Turpin?" Kenny interrupted. "Turpin, Turpin, Turpin. Your daddy Moses Turpin? Janitor up to the school?"

"No, sir. No relation. Lots of Turpins in Douglas."

"Wait a minute," Kenny said. "I do know you. Didn't you used to clean my mama's house?"

"No, sir, I did not. What I wanted to talk to you about is a missing persons case we're looking into." She handed Kenny the Polaroid. "Melodie Godwin. Went missing between Lee Road and the reservoir. Little over four weeks ago. Does she look familiar to you?"

"Right pretty girl," Kenny said and grunted as he passed the Polaroid back to the policewhore. "You might want to talk to them that lives right over yonder," he said and pointed to the house beyond the plot of pole beans. "They pose as Christians."

"Yes, sir. I've spoken with the Sewells. I've spoken with everybody that lives on Eden Road. Except for you."

"I've been in the hospital. First it was the diabetes, then I had the stroke. I just got back home week or two back. The church built this ramp for me, bought me this electric wheelchair. I'm just a cripple now. I used to be a deacon."

"Yes, sir, I understand. You own Kenny's Towing, also. Is that correct?"

Kenny shook his finger in a mock scold. "You've been checking up on me."

"Well, sir, not really, it's just that we checked with all the wrecker companies within a certain radius. Just in case Melodie's car had broken down."

"Melodie. That's a pretty name. Musical."

"Kenny's Towing is listed in the Yellow Pages as being located right here on Eden Road. Right in the middle of Melodie's route."

"Well, ma'am, as you can see for yourself, I ain't really in the towing business no more. I'm a cripple."

"Ms. Godwin went missing three days before you were admitted to the hospital."

"Godwin," Kenny said. "Godwin, Godwin, Godwin. God Win. God. Win. I didn't get no calls that day. And I would have remembered getting a call from somebody who was out there winning for The Lord."

"Are you aware of any kind of wreck or breakdown here on Eden Road around that time?"

"Can't say that I am. Not much traffic on this road. Just them cutting through to the reservoir."

Deputy Officer Turd Pan stood up and readied herself to leave. "I see you moved your roses."

"The county waterline would have run right through them."

"You did a good job. Hard to transplant this time of year with it being so hot." The pan of turds walked down the ramp, and wandered over to the roses.

"Did it at night," Kenny said. "That's the secret. You don't shock the roots that way. They're taking hold just fine. Blooming even."

"At night?"

Kenny watched as she shoved her flat nose into one of the blooms and took a deep whiff.

"I never would have thought of that. Church folk help you? No, I reckon church folk would be home in bed in the middle of the night."

"It was one of the neighbor boys. He helps me out. A good boy with good Christian folks. I pay him."

"Kyle Edwards?"

"Why, do you know what? I've never even asked that boy his name! Isn't that awful? I just call him boy. That's the way I was done when I was coming up."

The pan of turds pointed back behind the house. "That shed where you keep your tow truck?"

Kenny nodded.

"You know what my daddy did do? He owned a towing service. I'd love to see your rig."

"Oh I don't know about that. They's spiders and such in that shed. The air's bad in there. Been closed up so long."

"My daddy still keeps his hands in the business. Could maybe help you find a buyer for it if you're of a mind."

He noticed that she was laying on the just-folks Southern charm again. Kenny further noted that he had gone from being in complete control of the woman to being put on the defensive. The bodies the boy had dug up were in there. So was Melodie High-and-Mighty Godwin's car. For the love of Christ, Kenny wondered, what was it going to take to get this pan of turds away from his house?

"I reckon not. I reckon I'm not ready to sell it. I'm just a sentimental old man."

"I understand. You know what? I'm just going to peek at it real quick." And she disappeared around the side of the house. Kenny flicked on his chair and raced down the ramp as fast as he could. The side yard was a little lumpy, but as soon as he got to the smooth stone surface of the back patio, he was able to fly right up to the massive shed—a converted barn with a faded orange *GULF* sign hung above the massive double doors—which were already wide open. He'd told that boy to put the padlock back on.

The woman was running her fingers along the hood of his rig. "She's a beauty. 4300?"

Kenny nodded.

"'71?"

"1972 International 4300. Bought her new."

"A fine rig. Well, if you decide to sell it, let me know. You know what? It does smell bad in here."

"Probably a possum. They hole up in here sometimes and die. I'll get the boy to find it."

"Kyle?"

"That'd be the one."

"Is this your car here?" The policewhore fingered the gray tarpaulin covering Melodie Godwin's blue Chevelle Super Sport.

"Yes, ma'am."

"You interested in selling it at all?" Officer Turd Pan pulled up the tarp high enough for them both to get a glimpse of the powder blue paint.

"Officer Turpin, you know what? I wish you had took me up

AT THE END OF THE ROAD

on that glass of Kool-Aid. My sugar is dropping. If I don't get back inside this minute, I could go into a coma."

Officer Turd Pan dropped the tarp and said, "We'd better hurry then."

"I'm so dizzy. Could I get you to close up those doors? And put that lock on? The boy must have left it off."

IT WAS MIDNIGHT. THERE WAS NO MOON tonight, and Kyle decided to go through the cornfield. He didn't worry anymore about Soap Sally hiding in the corn. He'd seen the real Soap Sally. She wasn't hiding in the corn; she was chained up in the paralyzed man's attic. He knew now that Soap Sally was real—with the wild hair and the craziness in her eyes, and the bloodlust for little children. She even had needles on her finger-tips. But that wasn't right and Kyle knew it. Those weren't needles, they were just pop-tops. Her name was Melodie. And if Melodie really was Soap Sally, it was because the paralyzed man had turned her into Soap Sally. Just like he had turned Kyle into a zombie. He was changing all of them.

Kyle told himself over and over that the woman was Melodie. Melodie Godwin. That her mama missed her and wanted her to come back home. Melodie was caught up in all of this just like Kyle was caught up in it. She needed help. His help. And underneath it all, was the bad, bad feeling that all of this was his fault. It was because of him that the paralyzed man had caught her and changed her and turned her into Soap Sally. Because Kyle was riding his bicycle down the middle of the road, and she had to wreck herself to keep from killing him. She had sacrificed herself to save him. And now she was damned. Up ahead Kyle saw the dim green witch-light oozing out of the front window, and he reckoned him and Melodie were both damned.

HE GAVE KYLE THE ORANGE TOAST CHEE

crackers and the co-cola and told him to be quick, that they had a long night ahead of them.

Kyle wasn't scared like he thought he would be, going back up those stairs to see Melodie. He knew who she was now. She was just like him. That policewoman had shown him that. Kyle and Melodie were the same. They were both under his spell.

She was waiting for him when he got up there, real calm. She wasn't wearing those metal pop-tops on her fingers anymore, and she had made a kind of dress out of one of the garbage bags. She was just sitting there up against the pole she was chained to. Kyle could tell that they had both been thinking about each other and realized that they were the same. The crazy light had gone out of her eyes, and now Kyle could see the scared girl. She took the Coke and the crackers real gentle out of his hands, and used one of the old pull-rings to pry open the top on the Coke can because she didn't have fingernails, but Kyle could see that they were starting to grow back.

"Melodie?" he asked, keeping his voice real low.

She nodded and pointed at him and raised her eyebrows in question.

"I'm Kyle," he said. He pointed to the spot of wet scar tissue that bubbled her throat and asked, "Can you talk?"

She shook her head no.

"Did he do that to you?"

She nodded yes.

Kyle walked over to the pole and shook it. It was solid. So was the chain. Half-inch thick iron. "I'm going to help you get out of here."

Melodie smiled at him and touched the top of his head real soft. Then she touched real gentle right under the spot on his face where she had cut him.

"It's okay," he said. "I don't blame you."

Melodie pointed at herself, then to Kyle, and shook her head no.

He understood what she was saying. She was saying that she didn't blame him either.

"Boy!" It was him. Kyle could feel him controlling him. He had to go. He told Melodie that he would figure something out and left her up there.

DOWNSTAIRS, THERE WAS A LONG-handled bolt cutter and a set of car keys lying on the kitchen table. The paralyzed man told Kyle to pick them up, and that they were going out to the shed around back.

KYLE COULD SMELL THE BODIES EVEN though he had triple bagged them in plastic garbage bags.

Right next to the tow truck, there was a car under a piece of tarpaulin, and the paralyzed man told him to uncover it. Kyle recognized it right away. It was Melodie's car. He'd seen it in his dreams a thousand times.

"That colored policewhore been sniffing around here like I don't know what. Parking up from the house, spying. Got to tidy up. Got to get things right. First, pick up that broke piece of cinder block right over there. Good. Now, can you drive a car?"

"I ain't but ten."

"I could drive when I was ten. Drove a tractor. Your daddy never taught you?"

"Sometimes he lets me sit in his lap and turn the wheel."

"Sweet Jesus. Well, it's just as easy as pie."

KYLE WAS DRIVING MELODIE GODWIN'S
powder blue Chevelle SS straight down the middle of Eden Road.
It was two o'clock in the morning, and there were God-only-
knows-how-many dead bodies chopped up in trash bags in the
trunk. He was ten years old. The night air was cool as it streamed
in through the busted-out passenger window.

It was a straight shot down Eden Road to Sweetwater Reservoir. No turns, just the curves in the road. The paralyzed man
had told him how to find the little lever up under the front seat so
that he could slide the seat forward and his feet could reach the
pedals. He showed him the gas pedal and the brake pedal and said
that he should use the same foot for both of them, but Kyle found
himself wanting to use his left foot for the brake. He showed him
about changing the gears, but said not to worry too much about
it. The car was facing forward, so park and drive were the only
gears Kyle would need. He told him to just keep his foot on the
brake and let it off slow, to only give it gas real gentle like, then

put his foot right back over the brake, just resting it there. It was scary having all that metal under his control, but Kyle did okay.

And he said if Kyle got stopped by the police that he would see him in hell, because Kyle was as deep into this as he was.

Kyle kept the car dead in the middle of the road, going about five miles an hour. He had to stay in the middle, because when he got over to one side, it felt like the car was being pulled off the road and into the ditch. If Kyle wrecked it, that would be it. He only had one mile to go. He could do it.

Something was bothering his eyes. He had to squint them. It seemed like there was more light in the car than there had been a minute ago. The rearview mirror was throwing bright white light straight into his eyes. There was a car coming up behind him. It got right up on Kyle so that the car's interior was as bright as daytime. And that car just rode his rear end like that for what felt like a long time. That car couldn't have been more than two inches from his back bumper. That's when the blue lights started flashing.

I**T WAS LIKE A MONOCHROME KALEIDO**-scope, the blue strobes of light dancing around inside the car, bouncing off the rearview mirror and pulsing in his eyes. Kyle had seen this scenario on TV countless times, so he knew that he had two choices: he could hit the gas and try to outrun the police, or he could pull over to the side of the road and let the police have him. Even if Kyle had the skill to attempt to outrun a police car, he wouldn't have done it. Part of him was glad this was happening. He wanted to get caught. He wanted this to be over. Kyle figured that he would probably go to jail for everything he had done, but Melodie would be saved and the paralyzed man would be stopped. Although, he guessed the paralyzed man could say that Kyle was in it with him. What would his mama and daddy do to him after the police called them and said their little boy had been caught driving down Eden Road in the dead of night in a stolen car with dead bodies in the trunk? Bodies he had dug up out of the yard of a neighbor man?

Somehow Kyle managed to angle the car over to the side of the road without going into the ditch. He used his right foot on the brake and she stopped pretty easy. The police car stayed right up on him. They both sat there for a good long time. Kyle watched the blue lights bouncing off the landscape and disappearing into the blackness that the fire had created. In the little side mirror mounted on his door, Kyle saw the policeman open his door and step out. He stood there a minute writing something down, then he started walking up to the Chevelle. Behind the policeman, Kyle saw white light filling the horizon. Another car was coming. It had blue lights flashing too. And its siren was bleating. It was disturbingly loud in the night. The second police car blew by them like a bullet from a gun; the dust it kicked up from the road was caught in the headlights like red fog.

The policeman behind him ran back to his patrol car. Kyle saw him lean in the window and say something on his radio. Then he jumped in his car, hit the siren, and swerved around the Chevelle. He was gone as quick as that. Kyle sat there in the growing silence watching red dust sifting through the headlight beams, little bits of silica lighting up like diamonds.

There wasn't nothing left for him to do. Kyle took his foot off the brake and the car rolled forward.

Eden Road dead-ends at Mount Vernon Road, and the reservoir lies directly across. Kyle came to the stop sign, and even going as slow as he was, the car jerked to a rocking stop when he pushed down on the brake with his left foot. Kyle heard the bags in the trunk pitch forward. He looked both ways down Mount Vernon. It was deserted. He took his foot off the brake and the car nosed through the intersection right to the front gate of Sweetwater Reservoir.

After he pulled the gear lever to the park position, Kyle picked up the bolt cutter from next to him on the seat and got out of the car. At first he didn't think he was going to be able to cut through the metal padlock. Kyle brought all his strength to bear on the long handles of the bolt cutter and finally felt the mouth blades bite a little into the shackle, sink in a little more, and then pop through. Kyle tossed the broken lock into the backseat of the car just as he had been instructed.

He cut off the headlights, only then remembering that he was supposed to have done that before crossing over Mt. Vernon. A gravel road circled the outer perimeter of the reservoir. There was a quarter moon that night—enough light for him to see, but dark enough to remain hidden. Kyle was familiar with the reservoir and knew exactly the spot the paralyzed man had indicated. About a quarter-mile past the bait shop, one of the monolithic chunks of granite that dotted the shoreline was unusually flat. A favorite spot for fishermen, it was a thick, smooth slab that jutted far over the dark water.

Kyle aimed the car so it was pointing straight at the granite slab. He was about fifty yards back from it. The thing he had to be sure of was to give himself time and room to jump out of the car before it went over, but not so much that the vehicle might veer off course.

Kyle depressed the brake pedal and carefully shifted into park. He picked up the chunk of cinder block from the passenger side floorboard and placed it over the gas pedal. The weight of it pressed the gas pedal at least halfway to the floor. The engine roared like an angry beast, the sound of it disturbingly loud in the quiet night. Kyle felt the car lurch forward about an inch, straining to release all that pent-up energy. The paralyzed man had told him to leave the door wide open; that once he downshifted into drive, he'd have a good full second before the gear caught and the car took off. Just roll right on out, he'd told him. Don't try to jump and don't wait for the gear to catch, just roll right on out the door.

Kyle sat there making sure he had his actions planned out. He would have thought about it longer, but the protest from the engine was so loud that Kyle couldn't stand it anymore. He grabbed hold of the gear lever right above the steering column. He pulled it toward him to free it, then pulled downward. It wouldn't move. The paralyzed man had told him that might happen. The transmission won't like it, he had said. It's gonna strip the gears. But it ain't like she's gonna be selling it later. If it fights you, just use both your hands.

That's what he did. He wrapped both his hands around the gearshift and yanked like hell. There was a loud crunching sound and an immediate deep-throated grunt, and the car took off. Kyle rolled. He rolled right into the closed door. The sudden acceleration had slammed the door shut. His left arm was pinned between the seat and the door from the way he had rolled. By the time he righted himself, Kyle felt the front bumper bite violently into the granite slab. Then the car was in the air. He was surprised at how far out the car sailed. It seemed like it just floated there in midair. And when it hit the water, it wasn't very loud at all. It just sat there in the water, gently rocking, the engine dying. Kyle tried the door, but the water outside put up too much resistance. He was trapped.

He looked at the busted-out passenger window. Water was cresting over the opening. Kyle scrambled across the seat to crawl out the window, but his shoe got tangled under the parking brake. It was wedged tight. Kyle pulled, but it just wouldn't come free. Finally, he was able to slide his foot out of the shoe. When his foot was free, the water was gushing through the window. A nearly solid rectangular column of water. Kyle couldn't fight his way past it; the inward motion of it was too strong. The force of it swept him up and over the front seat. He was lodged up against the rear window in a pocket of air. The car was sinking nose first. Then it was underwater.

Everything was still and quiet, just the sound of the water lapping gently inside the car. Kyle was fine. He could breathe easy in the air pocket. He could stay just like he was and be fine, but he knew the air would run out after a while. He could feel his clothes weighing him down in the water. He could kick his shoeless foot with ease, but the other one dragged, so he pulled off the other shoe. He had to get back down to the front of the car and swim out the window. The air pocket was growing smaller and smaller, so pretty soon Kyle wouldn't have a choice. He could see air bubbling out around the seal of the rear window. The change in the pressure was causing the car to tilt over, to fall flat to the bottom. The interior would be completely full in just a few more seconds. Kyle held his breath as the car floated lazily toward the bottom. The weight of his clothes made it nearly impossible to swim, but his bare feet saved him. He propelled his body through the window, curved up, and broke through the surface.

Up top, crickets chirped in the dark night, and in his mind, Kyle could hear the paralyzed man laughing.

"THUM-THUM-THUM-THUM-THUM-THUM thum-thum. Thum-thum-thum-thum-thum-thum thum-thum. Wonder Womaaaaan!" Grace danced around her room, singing. Her little girl's voice carried down the hall, and into the kitchen, but her mother did not hear it. Her mother was preparing a chuck roast for that night's supper, but she wasn't thinking about the roast or enjoying the sound of her child's singing, as she once would have. And Grace knew it.

Grace missed her Wonder Woman doll. She didn't think of the doll as Wonder Woman, but as Diana Prince.

She had made up her mind to get the doll back. Kyle had told her that the bad man had it, the paralyzed man; and Kyle said he was going to get it back for her. But it had already been a long time. She believed in Kyle, but she just couldn't keep waiting for- ever. He spent all his time at the bad man's house, doing things for him. And now, not only had Grace lost her doll; she had lost her only other friend, her brother Kyle.

"Thum-thum-thum-thum-thum-thum thum-thum. Thum-thum-thum-thum-thum-thum thum-thum. Wonder Womaaaaan!"

Kyle didn't look right when he came back from that house. His eyes looked funny. There were dark circles under them and he just looked empty somehow. He used to talk and play and cut up with Grace, but not anymore. Sometimes he would just lie in the bed and do nothing. Just stare at the ceiling. He could pretend in front of Mama and Daddy pretty good, but Grace could tell that that was all it was—pretending. He just wasn't Kyle anymore. She didn't understand how Mama and Daddy couldn't see that he wasn't Kyle anymore, that he was just pretending to be Kyle. But a part of Grace realized that Mama and Daddy weren't really Mama and Daddy anymore, either. They were just pretending too. Mama still cooked dinner and gave Grace her bath, and made sure she brushed her teeth, but it was like a robot had replaced her mother. She was just doing those things out of habit. To Grace, it felt like her whole family had been replaced with robots that looked the same, but had no emotion.

Grace lay across her bed and sang softly now. She had made herself sad. What would Diana Prince do? What would Wonder Woman do to save her brother? Grace stood up, extended her arms, and began to spin. She imagined thunderbolts and a halo of ethereal light engulfing her body, transforming her. Grace imagined that she was beautiful like Diana Prince, with lustrous black hair and straight white teeth. And a big swollen chest like Diana had. She saw the way her older brothers looked at Diana Prince on the TV when she transformed into Wonder Woman. The way they stared at her bosom. Daddy stared at Mama like that too. Or he used to. Grace wanted men to look at her like that one day.

GRANT JERKINS

She went out to the laundry room, climbed on top of the humming dryer (it seemed like Mama did clothes every day), and
found a roll of duct tape on the utility shelf. It was hard, but Grace
used her teeth to tear off two small lengths of the shiny silver tape,
and wrapped a piece around each of her wrists. Grace decided that
the silver tape was made from Amazonium. Amazonium straight
from Paradise Island. These bracelets would protect her from any
force, no matter how great. They could even deflect bullets.

She returned the roll of tape and rummaged through the
crowded shelf until she found a length of clothesline. Grace gathered the rope into coils. This would be her Golden Lasso. Her
Lasso of Truth. She would throw it around the paralyzed man
and make him tell her what he had done with Kyle.

IT USED TO BE, SHE COULDN'T HAVE EVER tracked Kyle like this. He wouldn't have let her. But she spied on Kyle as he rummaged through Daddy's tool chest in the garage. She saw him take a little metal saw blade, tuck it into his sock, and cover it back with his jeans leg.

The sky was a blue true dream overhead as Grace followed Kyle into the cornfield, under the barbed wire, and to the green pond. He just sat at the green pond, throwing a rock into it every once in a while. Then it was back through the corn and emerging onto Eden Road directly in front of the paralyzed man's house. Kyle sat with the paralyzed man on his front porch, swinging softly on the porch swing. It looked like a boy spending a quiet summer morning with his grandfather. After a while, the paralyzed man drove his wheelchair through the door, and Kyle followed him into the house.

Grace wanted to see what they were doing inside the house. She looked at her duct tape bracelets, slammed the bracelets together, and believed the action formed a protective force field around her. She cut back up through the corn and emerged again in front of the Sewell house just as she had seen Kyle do last week. From the Sewells', Grace snuck through the remnants of the pole beans, over the muddy patch where the county had run the waterline, and up to the side window of the house. The window looked into the kitchen. The blinds were drawn, but they were cracked and in disrepair with plenty of gaps to peek through.

Inside, Kyle pulled something out of the refrigerator. It was a shot—like the kind they gave at the doctor's office. Kyle poked the needle high up on the paralyzed man's leg, and squirted whatever was in the shot inside the paralyzed man's thigh. Grace winced in empathy. She hated shots. After that, Kyle took a little glass bottle out of the refrigerator and filled up nine or ten of the little needles with the stuff from inside the bottle. He laid the needles out on a towel inside the refrigerator. Then Kyle took a Coca-Cola out of the refrigerator and reached down a pack of crackers from one of the cabinets. The paralyzed man said something to Kyle and pointed his finger at him while he said it. Kyle disappeared through an arched doorway, carrying the soda and crackers with him.

The paralyzed man sat there by himself in the kitchen. After a minute, he reached down into the little side satchel on his wheelchair. Grace saw something peeking out of the satchel that shocked her. It filled her with delight. Peeking out of the top, Grace saw the rich, glowing black hair of Diana Prince. Wonder Woman was in the satchel! She was right there! Grace was literally only a few feet away from her doll. But she might as well have been in another state. There was simply no way for her to walk in that house, reach into that satchel, and retrieve her doll. Not without being caught. But then something happened.

Fate, or maybe something more sinister, intervened. What happened next would set forth a sequence that would alter the course of Grace's life.

The paralyzed man pulled out and placed in his lap a dog-eared Bible, a very small pistol, even a pair of yellowed partials, before his hand found what it had been rooting around for: a small, sloping plastic jug with a wide mouth on top. When he pulled the jug out of the satchel, the wide mouth caught on Wonder Woman's leg and the doll tumbled out of the satchel and onto the floor. Grace's heart skipped a stitch. The paralyzed man hadn't noticed the doll. She was sure of it.

He pulled down the zipper on his pants and stuck his hand in and pulled out his wee-wee. It was wrinkly and white hairs sprouted out around it. He pushed his wee-wee inside the sloping jug. Grace saw that the mouth of the little plastic jug was made wide for this very purpose as it filled with the paralyzed man's dark urine. Grace had never before seen pee that dark. When he was finished, he held up the jug and inspected it before pouring it into the sink. One-handed, he rinsed out the jug and put it back in the satchel. He smoothed down the sparse strands of white hair on his head, and then he drove his wheelchair through the arched doorway toward the rear of the house. Wonder Woman lay unnoticed, faceup on the dirty linoleum floor, staring blankly at the ceiling.

ALTHOUGH GRACE CERTAINLY HAD A WARY respect for the paralyzed man, she was a girl, who, unlike her older brother Kyle, had no real fears. Sometimes she acted like a scared little girl, but that was mostly and usually an act for Kyle's benefit or to gain her daddy's attention. Ultimately, she was not prone to needless worry and agonizing indecision. Even at this young age, she was already growing toward a maturity that would have been marked by a tendency to action rather than planning. To her, the paralyzed man was like a snake or a spider—something best avoided, but she did not lie awake at night worrying about snakes and spiders.

Grace did, however, believe in hedging her bets. She banged together her duct tape bracelets—three times in rapid succession. And then she stole onto the front porch and carefully opened the door to the kitchen.

HE HAD HIT HER. AFTER ALL THESE MONTHS of worrying herself to death about it, Louise had finally got up her nerve to ask Boyd for a divorce. And he had hit her. In seventeen years of marriage, Boyd had barely ever raised his voice, and now this. She still couldn't believe it. He had actually hit her.

Louise looked at her reflection in the bathroom mirror. The eye was swollen about as much as it was going to, but the bruising had just set in. She had raised three boys, so she knew that it was the second and third day when a black eye looked its worst. She took out a tube of concealer and dabbed little blobs of it under her eye. She worked it in carefully and followed up with some foundation. She noticed that her hand was shaking. She realized that she wasn't sure if she was shaking out of fear or anger. The makeup worked—for now. When the bruising really set in, there would be no hiding it. But she just needed to get through tonight. She just needed to feed the kids their dinner and get them in bed. Without them realizing that something was wrong. She didn't want this affecting the children any more than necessary. But in the morning, after Boyd left for work, she was taking Grace and Kyle and she was leaving. Five minutes ago she had got off the phone with the apartment complex manager. If she brought cash with her, he had a unit she could have on the spot, no waiting. Louise had the cash. The phone service couldn't be turned on until next week, but the electric company could have a man out there tomorrow, and as long as Louise could pay the deposit on the spot, they'd get her power turned on. She assured them she could pay on the spot. She'd been saving for this moment well over six months. She had never imagined that it would happen like this. She had hoped that it would be more civilized, like it happened on *All My Children* or *As the World Turns*. It was always a sad situation, fraught with emotions running high, but it always ended in civilized acceptance. A scandal, not a crime.

Other than Jeannie, nobody she knew had ever gone through one, so Louise could only relate to divorce through books, movies, and soap operas. And country songs. She remembered Joan Crawford in the movie *Mildred Pierce*, and how Joan Crawford had divorced her husband and became rich by opening a chain of restaurants. And Mildred had affairs with rich handsome men. Men who wore suits and smoked cigarettes. Not men who worked for the post office and shoved a glob of Vaseline between their wives' legs on Saturday night after taking them out to eat at McDonald's.

Louise worked the foundation outward from her eye, blending it, wincing as she worked it outward in larger and larger circles. Then she remembered that everything hadn't come up roses for Mildred Pierce. The children. Mildred's daughters. The youngest had died of pneumonia. And the older girl, what was her name?

Veda. Her name had been Veda. A sweet, cute girl. Loving and devoted—until after the divorce. Then Veda had become ugly and mean natured. Running wild with boys. Faking a pregnancy to blackmail one boy. Then Veda ended up sleeping with her stepfather. Louise could not imagine a future in which it was possible for her sweet little Grace, her sweet little Wonder Woman, to end up in such a way.

Just get through tonight, Louise told herself. Just get through tonight, and tomorrow your life starts over. Tomorrow you'll leave Eden Road in the dust. Just get through tonight.

WITH THE DOOR AJAR, SHE COULD SEE that the kitchen was deserted. Her feet still planted squarely on the porch, Grace poked her head through the opening and listened. No sound came from any part of the house. She lifted her right foot over the threshold and planted it on the first square of soiled and foxed linoleum. There was a loud creak as the warped floorboards underneath announced her presence. With the utmost care, she brought her left foot forward to rest on the same square with her right. She stood there and listened—the coiled Lasso of Truth dangling from her left hand. No sounds. She advanced two more squares into the room; loud groans came from the floor both when she took her weight off the first spot and when she stepped onto the next. She stopped. Listened. Advanced. Wonder Woman lay isolated near the kitchen sink, just a yard-and-a-half away. Three more steps, six more squares to cross. The floor was less squeaky the farther she ventured into the kitchen, so she crossed quickly. Grace squatted down and snatched Diana

Prince from the dirty floor. In her heightened state of perception, Grace noted immediately that Diana's beautiful brown hair was knotted and tangled. This disturbed her, that in her absence, Diana Prince had been treated with such disregard. Grace took a second to pick at the tangles.

If Grace had simply scooped up her doll and run out the door, things might have turned out differently for her; but by the time she heard the hum of the electric motor, it was already too late. By the time she stood up, Kenny Ahearn was halfway across the kitchen. And before she could take her first step toward the door, the paralyzed man was there, his cumbersome metal wheelchair blocking her passage.

Grace stared up at him, her mouth slack, the pupils of her eyes dilated as though from drops of belladonna.

"IT'S OKAY, SWEET-GIRL," THE PARALYZED man said. "I wanted you to have that back."

Grace took a step backward.

"You want something to drink? Co-cola? I've got some Moon-Pies in the pantry there."

Grace shook her head.

"Why just look at you. Your eyes are big as dinner plates. You don't have to be scared of me, sweet-girl. I'm just Kenny Ahearn from across the road."

Grace wanted to believe him, but her mind returned to the day he had lured her up on his porch with this very same doll and grabbed her and wouldn't let her go until Kyle hit him in the head with a dirt clod.

"You're thinking about that time I held you in my lap, ain't you?"

Grace nodded.

"Sweetie, I am so sorry for doing that. I can't tell you. I didn't mean a thing by it. I was just mad at your brother, that's all that was. We've done got over that. We're friends now. Friends. Why, he comes over to visit with me just about every day. You can come over too. Any old time you want."

Grace took a step forward. "Can I go home now?"

"Why, I'm blocking your way, ain't I? 'Course you can go home." The wheelchair hummed and rolled forward just enough for Grace to pass. "Now you just remember that you're welcome here anytime." Grace slid past the paralyzed man like a climber traversing a vertical drop on Mt. Everest. She squeezed past him and emerged back out onto the porch. The paralyzed man followed.

"Oh yes, me and Kyle have us a good old time. Are you sure you don't want to stay a while and play with us?"

Grace conveniently forgot how Kyle had turned into something-other-than-Kyle since he had become friends with the paralyzed man, and instead she latched on to the thought of spending time with her brother again—through a shared friendship with Mr. Ahearn. She looked at the paralyzed man and realized that maybe that day he had grabbed her wasn't such a horrible thing. He'd let her go after a minute. And he wasn't stopping her now. Plus, he called her sweet-girl the way her paw-paw did before he went to live in the sky with Jesus. In fact, he looked like he could be somebody's paw-paw. Grace (not afraid, but pragmatic) decided that she should go on home for now, but also decided that she would come back. That she wanted to be a part of whatever was going on here.

"Bye-bye, sir."

"Sir? Sir? Why you can just call me Kenny."

Grace giggled. She had never called an adult by their first name. "Bye-bye, Kenny."

"Bye-bye, sweet-girl."

Grace took off down the steps and Kenny called out after her. "Sugar, what's your name?"

Grace turned around on the bottom step. "Grace."

"Grace, that rope you're holding there, that wouldn't happen to be a Golden Lasso, now would it? A Lasso of Truth?"

Grace beamed up at Kenny (for she had already forgotten her other name for him), her smile as wide open as her eyes had been earlier. She nodded with pride.

"You know what I bet? I bet you was gonna put that lasso around me and make me tell the truth. You were, weren't you?"

Grace nodded with a shy smile.

"You can if you want. I don't mind. Come on up here and I'll let you do it. Let's see if that lasso works."

Excited, Grace bound up the steps and followed Kenny back into the kitchen.

"ALRIGHT, NOW, I'M READY. YOU JUST GO ahead. Now don't be shy. I'm not."

Grace let Kenny hold one end of the clothesline in his hand while she walked around him, wrapping him.

"Alright, you just ask me anything."

On the spot, Grace couldn't think of anything to ask. She giggled and stared at the floor.

"It's hard to think of something sometimes. I know how it is. Tell you what," Kenny said, "why don't we put the lasso around you and I'll ask you some questions? How about that?"

That sounded like a fine idea to Grace. She unwrapped Kenny, and then wrapped herself in the rope.

"Now hold on a minute. I see you're wearing metal bracelets. Is that Amazonium?"

Grace nodded, again smiling with pride.

"It don't seem rightly fair that you should be wearing those.

The lasso might not work against Amazonium. Maybe you better take them off."

It took Grace a minute to work the duct tape off her wrists.

"That's right. Just stick them right there on the Frigidaire. Now, what we'll do, what we'll do is this. Let's see. I know. Tie one end of that rope to the doorknob there. Uh-huh. Good and tight. That's it. That's it. Now what can we do to make this more special? Let me think a minute. Just let me think. Oh, I know. I've got an idea."

KYLE HAD BROUGHT HER AN APPLE AND some Slim Jims from Mama's pantry. The paralyzed man never gave her anything but peanut butter crackers and Coca-Cola. She was busy eating what Kyle had brought while he worked at the chain.

He could see right away that it wasn't the right kind of saw. It was a hacksaw blade. Just the blade. About a foot long. He wasn't able to find the frame it was supposed to attach to. It was hard to hold the thin metal tight enough to get it to bite into the metal chain. But it was all he had, so he set to work.

Melodie watched him working on it, and every once in a while she would reach out and run her fingers over his hair. Kyle knew she wished she could talk to him, and that was her way of telling him thank you.

After a while, his arm got tired. It was numb, and his sawing motion got real slow. Melodie put her hand on his shoulder and held her other hand out for the saw. Kyle gave it to her. They both looked at the chain to see how much progress Kyle had made, but it wasn't much. The surface was scratched up some was all. Kyle wondered why Mr. Ahearn hadn't called up to him yet. He'd been at it at least twenty minutes. Usually, if Kyle was up here more than a minute or two he started hollering up at him. Saying things like "Leave that dirty whore alone, boy."

Melodie set to it. Her fingers were better now, with new fingernails budding from the beds. In fact, she was doing a better job with the saw blade than Kyle had. She pulled and pushed the saw in long, even strokes. It didn't slide and skip around like it had when Kyle had been sawing. Slow and even. Kyle could tell that the blade had bit into the metal now. Probably just broke through the heavily oxidized chrome finish, but it was progress. She stopped one time to readjust the garbage bag she was wearing to cover her nakedness. Kyle looked away.

All he could think about was why hadn't the paralyzed man called up after him yet. Maybe he was sneaking up here to catch them. Kyle decided to leave Melodie to it. He didn't want them to get caught, so he went on back downstairs.

KYLE GOT TO THE BOTTOM AND IT WAS
dead quiet down there. He looked into the living room and didn't
see anything. He looked to the little arch leading into the kitchen
and couldn't sense any kind of movement there. In the back of his
mind Kyle was thinking maybe he had had another stroke. Or
that maybe he couldn't get to his medicine needles in time and the
diabetes had killed him. Kyle walked into the kitchen, hoping like
hell that he would find him in there, sprawled out in his chair,
cold and dead. But that's not what he found. Not at all.

Grace was tied up to the door. She was sitting down, and a
length of rope pinned her hands up over her head to the doorknob.
There were two pieces of duct tape over her mouth, crisscrossed
like an X. She wasn't crying, but Kyle could see where the tears had
dried. Her Wonder Woman doll was lying on the floor next to her.

He untied her hands and pulled the tape off her mouth as
gentle as he could. "Are you okay?" he asked her, but she didn't
answer him.

There was a little blue, thumb-shaped bruise just under her jaw.

"What did he do to you?"

She still didn't say anything.

Kyle picked up her doll and put it in her hand. He walked her out onto the porch and down the ramp. They crossed over Eden Road and into the corn. Kyle took his sister to the green pond and they sat out there throwing rocks into the stagnant water the rest of the day. He tried talking to her, but she never would answer him. She would look at her doll sometimes and stroke its hair.

When they went home that evening, neither Mama nor Daddy neither one noticed that something was wrong with Grace. They were far away, not living in their own bodies. Daddy kept his face hidden behind the newspaper, and Mama kept her face poked over the pots simmering on the stove. In the steam and the bright kitchen light, Kyle could see that something was wrong with Mama's eye. Something was off.

At dinner, they just stared down into their plates. Neither one of his parents talked to Grace or him except to give short little mechanical directions. Wash your hands. Sit down. Wipe your mouth. And with Jason and Wade at vacation Bible school, the house was quieter than Kyle had ever heard it.

Kyle didn't know it yet, but his mother and father's worlds had changed that day too. Like Kyle and Grace, they would never be the same. Nobody on Eden Road was ever going to be the same. They had all been cast out.

Kyle would never come to know what the paralyzed man had done to Grace that day. Ultimately, he came to thank God for sparing him that knowledge.

During the course of the next week, Grace didn't say a single word, and when she did begin to talk again, she wouldn't mention what had happened to her. But the arc of her life had been altered. She was never the same girl. She and Kyle never played much together after that. She kept to herself mostly. Mama took her to doctors, and they gave her pills to help ease her mind.

She began sneaking cigarettes by the time she was nine. She was caught smoking pot at school when she was twelve. When she started in junior high, Grace got boy crazy. She would sneak off in the middle of the night to be with them. Older boys. Men sometimes. She was expelled from high school for drinking. The police brought her home one night after the boy she was with was arrested for selling heroin. Finally, when she was seventeen, Grace ran away with a thirty-two-year-old man named Lucius Allen. Her mother, (who, frankly, had given up on Grace by then) reported her missing to the authorities, and the police treated it as an abduction. Lucius Allen had a criminal record that included two arrests for pimping. They never found Lucius Allen, and Grace never again contacted her family.

What became of her during the intervening years, no one will ever know, but ultimately, at the age of thirty-seven, Grace Edwards slid silently away from this world in a downtown Atlanta hotel room, a mixture of methamphetamine, Xanax, and vodka carrying her pragmatic, unafraid little girl's soul back to Eden.

THE
SERVANT OF
THE ASH

HER SERGEANT CALLED HER AT HOME just as she was getting dressed for her shift. He knew that Dana had taken the case to heart and figured that she would want to be there when they pulled the vehicle out. She put on her uniform and headed for the reservoir. A hobby fisherman had spotted an oil slick not too far off from the shore. He was a retired butcher and he fished for carp three days a week—each time from his favorite spot: a giant slab of granite that jutted up and out over the water. He knew the reservoir, and in particular, he knew that spot on the reservoir like he knew tenderloin from short loin. The oil was bubbling up from the bottom, he had said. And there was a shadow down there that had never been there before. It was a car, he had said. See if I ain't right, he'd said. Just see.

They saw. He'd been right. With Sweetwater Reservoir being Melodie Godwin's final destination, the consensus was that they would be dragging out a powder blue 1972 Chevrolet Chevelle

Super Sport with Ms. Godwin's remains lodged inside. How Melodie Godwin had managed to drive her car off a rock cliff and into the reservoir in broad daylight without anyone witnessing it was a question for another day.

Dana saw the cluster of sheriff's department vehicles just beyond the bait shop and parked her cruiser amongst them. To the left of the rock slab, the contracted diver was just coming out of the water after having attached the towing wench to the submerged car. No one was fishing today; a crowd of about forty people stretched in a half circle from the shoreline.

Dana's heart sank when she saw Mrs. Godwin and Melodie's oldest sister, Deanna Wilson, at the front of the gathering. Who in their right mind would have called the family? To what purpose? If it wasn't Melodie's car, then the family would have gone through this ordeal for nothing. They would have come here feeling that closure was imminent, already allowing themselves to grieve the death of their loved one, to witness this final formality, only to have it snatched away and find themselves shoved back into the lingering discomfort of uncertainty.

And if it was Melodie's car, well then Melodie's mother was about to see firsthand what the body of her daughter would look like after four weeks submerged underwater.

Dana had never seen such a sight herself, but the old-timers had told her tales. Racially motivated crimes had once been common in Douglas County (still were, really), and in the early 60s as the dams were being completed, this man-made lake (officially the George H. Sparks Reservoir) had been a hot spot to dispose of the bodies of black men killed by whites over rage-filled drunken weekends and sober Sundays of righteousness. After about a week underwater, the corpses swelled with gases and floated to the surface, dragging weighted ropes beneath them. Bodies in water decompose at a much faster rate than those underground, but slower than those exposed to air. Things nibble at bodies underwater. Catfish are bad about that. With Melodie (assuming this was indeed her car), if there was an air pocket trapped in the interior with the body, the putrefaction could be quite ugly. Melodie's mother did not need the last image of her daughter to be any of those eventualities.

Dana watched the lake water gush and drain out of the car as it emerged. The crime scene photographer snapped pictures as the extraction progressed. Dana couldn't see the plates yet, but it was a 1972 powder blue Chevelle SS. No question, this was Melodie Godwin's car. As soon as the vehicle was completely out of the water, Dana scooted behind the photographer and matched the license plate numbers with what she had written in her notebook. They were an exact match.

She was disappointed.

Dana was ashamed that the emotion she felt the strongest in this moment was disappointment. She didn't fully understand why she had taken Melodie's disappearance to heart like she had. Perhaps it was simply because everybody else was so eager to file it away. Another fast girl living a fast life up and disappeared. So what? But it had meant more than that for Dana, and she felt compelled to keep at it.

Dana didn't typically like to look too deeply into herself for the impetus behind her motivations. If someone were to ask her why she had become a sheriff's deputy officer in the first place, she would not know how to answer. She of course could answer in some generic fashion, but in her heart she did not know what had compelled her to follow this course in life. A desire to help others? Sure. Racial pride? Perhaps. A strong sense of justice in an unjust world? Maybe. Something had formed her to be the way she was, and Dana saw no benefit in digging that something out. So, when the notion to enter law enforcement had entered her mind, Dana had simply put her head down and plowed forward. She did not question it. And when her heart told her to not give up on Melodie Godwin, she just kept pushing forward.

No, she had not given up, and now here she was, and after this last dose of ugliness, Melodie's family would finally find some peace, and Dana herself would also find some measure of peace. The steady spiritual itch that had been the unexplained disappearance of Melodie Godwin was now relieved. So why did she feel disappointed? Was it just her ego? Dana was ashamed to acknowledge to herself that it was nothing more profound than wounded pride. She was disappointed in herself for coming at this thing from the wrong angle. She had been certain that Melodie had disappeared on Eden Road. Yes, she had been pleased with herself for finding that safety glass that otherwise would have sunk into the mud with the next good rain. And the boy. Kyle. Dana had centered in on the boy from nothing more than a broken glance through an open door. She was prideful of her instinct to follow up with the boy. And she had grown certain that Kyle had some knowledge about Melodie, but was too scared to tell.

THE SHERIFF WRESTED THE DRIVER SIDE
door open while Dana's friend, Senior Deputy Ben Hughes, opened the passenger door on the other side. The metal joints had set up underwater and groaned in protest at being so rudely made to bend again. Dana couldn't see because the men's bodies blocked the view into the car's interior. They emerged from the car at the same time, and Dana could see straight through it. The front was empty. The backseat too was empty. There was no body. The car was empty, but Dana knew this was not an entirely worrisome occurrence. Assuming she could swim, Melodie very well could have managed to escape from the car, but still drowned. After a crash like that, the driver and any occupants are typically disoriented, unable to tell up from down, unable to swim to the surface. The absence of the passenger side window seemed to confirm that Melodie had at least managed to escape from the car, but it also caused Dana to think again about the auto glass she'd found in the ditch on Eden Road.

Dana glanced over at Mrs. Godwin. The look of sad puzzlement on the woman's face was heartbreaking.

The sheriff returned to the front of the car, leaned in, and pulled the keys from the ignition with his gloved hand. At the rear of the car, he used the key to open the trunk. The sheriff pulled out two black trash bags, tightly knotted at the tops. Ben Hughes reached in and pulled out two more. Ben took out a pocketknife and readied to slit one bag open, but the sheriff waved him off. Both men stepped back and allowed the photographer to take pictures of the unopened bags. The sheriff got out his own pocketknife and indicated with his beefy hand for the senior deputy to proceed as well. Going against most anybody's interpretation of correct crime scene protocol, they split the bags open. Body parts spilled out from the bags like unfortunate prey from a gutted shark's belly. The sheriff lurched backward, falling on his backside. He covered his mouth as he coughed and choked. Ben ran to the water's edge and vomited. Dana heard Melodie's sister scream, and looked up to see Mrs. Godwin collapse to the ground.

After a minute, the odor from the bodies carried to Dana. Diluted with air, she knew that she was getting only a fraction of what the two men had been exposed to. The odor made her think of the dead possum she had smelled in the garage on Eden Road, only worse. Dana noted that some of the remains were essentially skeletal, while some held on to flesh in varying stages of putrefaction.

Dana joined two of her fellow deputies who, like her, had only been observing, and began urging the onlookers away from the crime scene, instructing them to leave the area completely. Dana retrieved a roll of crime scene tape from her vehicle and worked with another deputy to cordon off the area. She busied herself and made herself useful, but her primary interest was in watching the scene unfold and develop. The Georgia Bureau of Investigation would likely take an interest in this, so Dana felt an urgency to see as much as she could while the sheriff's department was still in control.

She saw Ben Hughes begin bagging evidence from inside the car, and went over to assist him. As he bagged and tagged the items, Dana ran them to the trunk of the sheriff's cruiser. The items were of no real interest, trash from the floorboards mostly, but also a pair of bolt cutters and a broken chunk of cinder block.

Waiting for the next item to be handed out to her, Dana noted that the front seat of the vehicle was adjusted to its uppermost forward position, leaving a space too small for a typical adult to wedge into. Melodie Godwin was a tall girl. In family photographs, she towered over her mother and sisters.

Ben was holding out the next evidence bag. Dana took it. It was a pair of sneakers. Child size. Boys'.

THEY WERE AT THE FREE CLINIC IN AT-
lanta. After the first month/last month deposit on the apartment
and the utilities deposits, there just wasn't enough left over to pay
for a regular doctor. At least she had the car. It was hers, free and
clear, and in her name.

Kyle was off. He just wasn't right. He just wasn't Kyle anymore. He almost seemed like he was sleepwalking. But that didn't
bother Louise. She figured it was to be expected. Because of the
separation. The soon-to-be divorce. The boy was just naturally
upset, maybe even a little depressed.

But whatever was wrong with Grace was not something natural. Grace had not spoken a word, had not even made a sound in
the week since Louise had left her husband.

BOYD HAD TO LEAVE THE HOUSE AT 5:45
every morning to be at the mail-processing plant on time. As
soon as he was gone the morning after he hit her, Louise had

woken up Kyle and Grace and told them to get dressed. She packed up her things while the kids were getting ready. After that, she sat them down in front of the TV with bowls of milk and cereal while she went to their room and packed up clothes for them. She loaded up the car, then went back inside to get the kids, thankful that Wade and Jason were away at vacation Bible school. Inside, she found Kyle sitting by himself watching cartoons.

"Kyle, where's your sister?"

Kyle looked around as if just now realizing Grace wasn't there. "I don't know, Mama."

Louise checked in the bathroom, and then in all the rooms in the house. "Kyle, she must have gone outside to play, can you go out and find her for me? We've got to go. We've got a lot to do today."

Kyle went outside, and Louise could hear his voice outside calling his sister's name. Louise took her makeup bag out of her purse and went back to the bathroom mirror to doctor her eye some more. The bruising had deepened overnight, and now the concealer just couldn't quite cover it. As she worked the makeup into her skin, she stopped thinking for a minute. No thoughts at all. It was a small blessing. Then movement behind her drew her forward again, and she looked at Kyle reflected behind her in the mirror.

"I can't find her anywhere. She won't answer me."

Louise threw her paraphernalia back in the bag and zipped it. This was exactly the kind of complication she didn't need today. Louise stomped outside and began to call for her child. She yelled out promises of spankings and crape myrtle switches, but to no result. Louise stood there in the gravel driveway, ready to cry in frustration, Kyle standing next to her. And then there was a small rustling sound, and Grace emerged from the withering corn. Louise ran up to the girl and shook her roughly by the shoulders.

"Where have you been? Why didn't you answer me? You always, always answer your mother. Now get in the car. Both of you."

Louise forced herself to calm down once she was on the road with the children. It was going to be hard enough on them, and she wanted to make this transition less traumatic if possible. "We're going on a trip," she said to them. "Don't that sound like fun? Grace, don't that sound like fun?" But Grace didn't answer. Louise pressed forward with the speech she had rehearsed. About how much fun this was going to be.

IF LOUISE HAD BEEN ABLE TO THINK clearly at any point over the last week, she would have almost certainly noticed that Grace's becoming mute had not been concurrent with them leaving Boyd, but had started the day prior to that. So, when the doctor at the clinic, a short Indian man with dark skin and an odor Louise found objectionable, asked her when the problem started, she answered as truthfully as she could.

"I see," the doctor said in a thick accent. "And your eye, Mrs. Edwards? What can you tell me about that?"

"I don't understand," Louise said, although she understood perfectly well and they both knew it.

"Did your husband hit you?"

"You don't understand. Boyd has never . . . It's complicated."

"I understand very well. With your permission, I would like to talk to Grace alone. The nurse will remain present, of course, but oftentimes a child will open up more readily without the parent present. It is for the best."

"She lost her doll. We can't find it anywhere. I think that she's just upset about that. I bet that's all it is."

"Let me examine her. Let me talk to her."

The doctor opened the door of the exam room and called for a nurse. He looked to Louise and motioned toward the waiting room. "I will take good care of your little girl. It is for the best."

With a feeling of dread, Louise stood up and walked out of the exam room, leaving Grace perched atop the vinyl examination table that was covered with stark white butcher paper that crinkled whenever she moved.

Louise took her seat next to Kyle in the waiting room. She was certain that Grace was going to be okay. She had just now remembered about that doll. It had been lost for a while now, but Louise just bet that was what was wrong with Grace. That was all it was. She realized now that she had made a mistake in coming here. She looked around the waiting room and saw that the people who surrounded them were not the kind of people Louise was used to being around. To her, they looked disease ridden. When they got back to the apartment, Louise would make both of the kids take a good hot bath. So many changes in her life in such a short time. She was overwhelmed. It was all just too much. She hoped that Wade and Jason would adjust okay. She was going to call Boyd tonight and talk about visitation. Maybe every other weekend Wade and Jason could stay with her, and Grace and Kyle could stay with their father. The children had to be the priority. Of course, Louise still had to find a full-time job. The money was already running low. She might have to find a lawyer to set up child support payments. Surely Boyd would do the right thing without her having to get a lawyer.

Louise looked around the waiting room and stared at a Mexican man who appeared to have a cancerous growth eating away at one of his nostrils. Maybe she had made a mistake. Maybe life on Eden Road wasn't so bad. Maybe Boyd could change. Maybe there was a chance that they could patch things up. For the children. Kyle would need a father's presence.

"Mrs. Edwards?"

Louise looked up at the beckoning nurse and followed her back to the exam room. Grace sat in the same spot on the exam table with a sucker in her mouth that had stained her lips a deep neon blue. One of those sugar-free safety lollipops with the soft loop handle instead of a stick. She looked as though she hadn't moved, but the white butcher paper was now creased and wrinkled and a little bit dirty.

"I can see nothing physically that would explain your daughter's mute state. She communicates quite readily with head movements and facial gestures."

"So she's okay?"

"Does your husband ever hit the children? Touch them?"

"No. I don't understand."

"While there is nothing physically wrong with her vocal cords, Grace indeed has undergone a physical trauma. And perhaps more importantly, a psychological one."

Louise stared at the doctor. She was having trouble following his words. Not because of the accent, but because her mind could not comprehend the concept that he was trying to convey to her.

"I examined your daughter, Mrs. Edwards, and I found evidence of trauma to Grace's genital area."

"What?" Louise asked. It was the only response she could manage.

"There was no physical evidence to collect, semen I mean, because it's been too many days. And, frankly, I think an object was used. There were some abrasions to her inner thighs. Some tearing internally."

Louise just could not comprehend what this man was saying to her. His words echoed in her mind. Such harsh, hateful words. She looked at the doctor and said, "Boyd would never . . ."

"I'm afraid that I'm required by law to report this."

"No!" Louise shouted. "She lost her doll. You don't understand. She loved that doll. She's just upset. She'll grow out of it."

The doctor folded his brown hands under his chin in thoughtful repose. Louise could smell him. His cultural odor mingled with antiseptic. She wanted to vomit.

"Mrs. Edwards, you can live with someone your whole life and never even scratch the surface of who they really are. Unless he admits it, or unless Grace speaks up, his crime will almost certainly go unpunished. Unless, of course, you believe in Karma. There is no real evidence. Still, it must be reported to DFACS."

"D-facts?"

"The Division of Family and Children Services."

IN THE CAR, TEARS STREAKED LOUISE'S face, and her vision blurred so that she had trouble seeing the traffic. She had failed Grace. That was all she could think. She had failed Grace. She had waited too long to leave Boyd. Maybe she wasn't being selfish by leaving him. Maybe she wasn't thinking of only herself. Maybe some maternal instinct deep inside her had urged her to take the youngest children and leave. But she waited too long to obey that instinct.

"Mama," Kyle said. "Are you okay?"

When Louise looked at her son, she saw two images of him through the prism of tears.

"Kyle, has your father ever touched you?"

THE TICKING OF THE CLOCKS IN THE EMPTY house soothed him.

Boyd Edwards was a profoundly confused man. Confused and disturbed at what he had found lurking inside himself, and even more disturbed that forces outside him had converged to disrupt his life so completely. With the boys at Bible camp, the house was empty, the comforting sound of the ticking clocks his only accompaniment while Boyd read (yet again) the note his wife had left behind when she took his two youngest children and deserted him.

Yes, he had hit Louise, so he had to face that in himself. He had to acknowledge to himself that, yes, he was capable of that. The truth was that he didn't even remember having done it. When Louise had told him that she wanted a separation, Boyd's mind had raced through all the implications of that word, then he had blacked out for just a second. When he came back to himself, Louise was crying, her hands covering her face.

Secretly, Boyd did not believe in God or Jesus Christ. He saw little difference between the idea of a God who healed the sick and rose from the dead, and stories they told children about an immortal man in a red suit who drove flying reindeer around the globe to deliver presents. Nonetheless, Boyd lived a Christian life, and he thought of himself as a Christian. As such, there were certain expectations placed on him, and certain expectations he placed on himself. Boyd may not have been a true believer, but he truly believed in Christian values. Eden Road. He had purposefully brought his family here to grow. This was his Garden of Eden. Louise was his Eve. The rural Georgia where he had been raised was largely gone now, but Boyd had found Eden Road—a little piece of what was. And just as there had been a corrupting serpent in the original garden, corruption had been brought here as well. But who had brought it?

Louise had said that he just used her for sex. Well, who was he supposed to use?

A separation. It had caught him by utter surprise. He thought that he and Louise were happy together. Until just about a week ago, Boyd had certainly been happy. Well, not happy, that was not his nature; and not even content, for contentment was not in his nature either; but certainly he was satisfied. Or, again, he had been until a week ago. In fact, he had already been well on his way to finding a way of being satisfied with his new situation in life— until the social worker showed up at his door accusing him of molesting his little girl.

It just didn't make sense. Someone had touched his little girl. It had not been him. His wife had left him and his daughter had been molested. Boyd's mind raced past the ticking of the clocks, and he was almost grateful for the loud knocking at the door that forced him to get up.

DANA DROVE STRAIGHT FROM THE CRIME
scene at the reservoir to the Edwards house. Her gut had told her
that Kyle Edwards was involved in this, and the evidence she observed confirmed it. But not enough. A pair of sneakers and a car
seat adjusted all the way forward was not enough to point the finger at Kyle. It was not enough for her to say his name to the sheriff
or the GBI, to thrust Kyle Edwards forward as the first and only
lead in a multiple homicide.

But it was far, far too much to let go.

KYLE'S FATHER ANSWERED THE DOOR,
and rather than invite her in, he stepped out onto the front porch
with her.

"Yes, ma'am?"

"Boyd Edwards? Father of Kyle Edwards?"

"Yes, ma'am, I'm Kyle's father. Don't worry. He's safe."

"Why wouldn't he be safe?"

"I reckon you all figure a man who would violate his own daughter might not stop with just girls."

"Sir, I don't understand what you're telling me. I need to speak to your son."

"He's gone. My wife took him and my daughter. She left me."

"Sir, what happened to your daughter? Can you tell me that?"

"They say I molested her. As you damn well know."

Dana took a step back. She just realized that she could very well be standing face-to-face with the man who killed Melodie Godwin.

"Sir, where has your wife taken them?"

"I don't know. I'm the bad guy, remember?"

"Sir, I'm sorry to have disturbed you. And I'm sorry that trouble has come to your family."

Dana got back into her patrol car, turned around, and headed back up the driveway. The field of corn to her right had been picked, and the stalks were already turning brown and withering. Dana didn't want Boyd Edwards to see her using the radio, so she waited until she pulled back onto Eden Road before calling dispatch. She asked to be patched straight through to the sergeant. Jesus, how could she have been so stupid? Was it ego again? If Boyd Edwards was responsible for Melodie Godwin and whoever else's bodies that were in that car, then she had just personally alerted a murderer that the authorities were interested in him. She had to let the others know.

To her left, Dana saw Kenny Ahearn sitting out on his porch, and she immediately thought of that day in his storage barn, how nervous he had been to have her snooping around. The car under the tarp, the flash of powder blue paint, the smell of the dead possum.

SHE SWUNG HER VEHICLE INTO AHEARN'S
drive; her mind was racing, trying to put all this together before
she made another stupid mistake. A public mistake. She picked up
the radio, keyed the mic, and said into it, "Dispatch, cancel that
last request."

Dana walked up the ramp. "Mr. Ahearn, how are you today, sir?"

"Just fine, Officer, just fine."

"Sir, this is rather embarrassing, but do you remember the
other week I was out here talking to you?"

"'Course I do."

"Well, sir, I misplaced my notepad that day, and I'm pretty
certain that I might have left it in your storage shed out back
there."

"Why don't you run back there and check? I'm sure it's not
locked. That boy never locks it back."

"Thank you, sir." Dana noted the dramatic change in Mr.
Ahearn's disposition. He seemed to welcome her presence. In the

shed, Dana saw immediately that the car was no longer there, the tarp lay folded neatly in the corner. There was a faint smell of bleach, and the concrete floor had been scrubbed clean. That was all she needed to see.

OUT FRONT, MR. AHEARN ASKED, "DID YOU find what you were looking for?"

"'Fraid not. But thank you." She didn't ask about the car, if it had been sold, or maybe stolen. She did not want to arouse suspicion any more than she already had. She wanted to talk to Kyle. She still needed to come forward with her sergeant, but there was no urgency now. Melodie Godwin was dead. She wasn't going to get any deader. Best to get her facts straight. Be sure. But first she just wanted to talk to Kyle. She would check with the utility companies. If Louise Edwards was using her real name, it shouldn't be a problem. If something had happened to the little girl, there would be a case open at DFACS. They were traceable. She would find Kyle.

"Take care now," Kenny Ahearn called out as Dana got back into her vehicle.

THE BOYS HAD FORCED KYLE TO A CORner. It was fight or flight time, and Kyle could see no more opportunities for flight.

Kyle did not like this new world. Where once he had the woods and pasture to explore, now he had asphalt and alleys. He did not belong here, and the other kids could smell that wrongness on him. It was safer to sit inside the apartment and watch TV, but that was not in Kyle's nature. He had to be outside. To be able to think, to try and comprehend what had happened to him and his family, he had to be outside.

His mother had taken him away from Eden Road. Away from his father. His father seldom talked to Kyle, and in fact, Kyle felt that he barely knew the man, but, still, he was all Kyle had ever known. His brothers put most of their energy into avoiding Kyle, so, again, it was not that he missed them so much as he missed the idea of them. The constancy of them.

He was glad to be away from the paralyzed man. Now he was

in a place where that man could no longer influence him, no longer control him. Already, Kyle felt better in that regard. He felt relieved that he no longer had to bear the burden of not knowing what new obscenity each day would bring. The paralyzed man could not find him here.

Kyle did not know what Kenny Ahearn had done to Grace. In fact, his mind would not even allow itself to speculate in that direction. He had gone with his mother today to take Grace to the clinic, and when they were finished there, his mother had been crying and Grace still would not speak. And Mama had looked at him and asked Kyle if his daddy ever touched him. Kyle knew instinctively just what she meant. He knew about the men who touched little kids and realized that his mama thought his daddy might be one of those nasty men.

Just a little while ago, he had been sitting on the couch with Grace while their mother lay down to take a nap. Grace had reached over and grabbed hold of Kyle's hand. She had looked at him, and she had spoken to him. Her voice was just a tiny whisper. "I'm scared, Kyle," she had said. "I'm scared he's gonna come get me. You have to save me."

THE FIRST BOY FELL IN BEHIND HIM WHILE
Kyle was walking through the apartment complex. There were so many people here. And so many different kinds of people. Kyle wondered how he could get back to Eden Road. How could he stop the paralyzed man? Would Grace be okay again if he could somehow put an end to Kenny Ahearn? He needed to go back. There was Melodie Godwin. Who was going to save her? If Kyle could stop Mr. Ahearn, then he could save Melodie. It was his fault that Melodie had run up against the paralyzed man in the first place. It was his fault that Grace had run up against him too. But was it too late to save Grace? Would the knowledge that Kyle had put an end to it soothe Grace's mind?

A second and then a third boy fell in line with the first. They were older than Kyle. They could tell he was out of place. Kyle pretended that he was unaware of them, but tried to walk to a place of safety. A fourth and a fifth boy joined the pack, and Kyle knew that he had been targeted.

And how was it possible to put an end to it? What could Kyle do that he had not already done? He was just a boy.

Kyle had been heading toward the road outside the complex. It was a busy access road that fed into the highway. Cars and trucks flew down it. If he could cross it, there was a bus station and shopping plaza that sprawled along the far side. But Kyle saw too late that a steep drainage ravine separated the apartment complex from the access road. Kyle peered down into the ravine. It was deep, and the bottom was littered with weeds and jagged chunks of construction debris. The side of the ravine was a sharp, dangerous drop, but Kyle could get down it with little problem. The banks leading down into Sweetwater Creek were steeper. The true problem was that the far side was a flat concrete wall that supported the access road. It was a sheer vertical plane. If he went down into the ravine, he would be trapped. And he would be completely out of sight down there. The boys could do anything they wanted and not be seen.

"Hey, man, you got a quarter?"

Kyle turned around. The biggest boy, about sixteen, had long greasy black hair and sparse patches of kinky beard sprouted from his face. He was just inches away, threateningly close. The others hung back, watching the drama unfold. This was where Kyle would be tested.

"No," Kyle said. "No, I sure don't."

"Aw man, it's just a quarter. C'mon."

"I don't have any money."

"You're not lying to me, are you?"

Kyle shook his head.

"Turn your pockets out."

Kyle shook his head.

"What? Are you telling me no? You're telling me no?" The greasy-haired boy looked back to his friends. "This kid just told me no." He turned back to Kyle. The playfully threatening tone was gone, now it was a full threat of impending violence. "Turn out your pockets, motherfucker. Right now."

Kyle did as he was told. And when he pulled his pockets inside out, he was plainly concealing something in his right hand.

"Open your goddamn hand before I break it open."

Kyle opened his hand. One of the boys in back whistled appreciatively. Kyle was holding the silver dollar that Grace had given him in the treasure hunt game. He'd had ample opportunity to spend it, but Kyle had enjoyed just holding it, the comforting heft of it in his pocket. It felt good to him.

"Fuck," the biggest boy said. "That's a standing liberty. Solid silver. We can get ten bucks for that at the pawnshop. No sweat. Give it to me."

Kyle shook his head. He wasn't really thinking about self-preservation anymore; he had simply decided that the dollar was his, and he was not going to give it up without a fight. The biggest boy pulled a knife from his pocket. It was a butterfly knife. The boy's wrist snapped with three sharp jerks, and the metal parts of the knife made wicked clicking sounds as they unfolded. All five of the boys advanced toward him.

Kyle looked behind himself into the deep ravine, and there, amidst the warped sheet metal and broken slabs of crumbling concrete, he saw something familiar. Kyle shoved the silver dollar back in his pocket. He jumped into the ravine.

From the bottom, Kyle saw the boys crest the brink and begin to carefully pick their way down the steep incline. Kyle had run down it. The earth was dry and no weeds grew on the bank and so he knew there were no roots to hold the ground in place. The earth shifted and gave way with each step. Running was the best way to cover such ground. You kept moving before the ground had a chance to shift. But the boys didn't know that. So they picked their way slowly, lest they take an unforgiving tumble into the cast-off concrete and metal.

Kyle set to work gathering up the sharp rigid stalks of blood-weed that he had spotted on the marshy bottom amidst the debris. He stacked a small cord of it atop a projecting cement slab with steel rods twisting out of it. Kyle climbed atop. He made quick work to prepare his bloodweed javelins. Each one was about six or seven feet long. He shook the sand and dirt off the bottom to expose the wickedly sharp taproot. He then stripped the stalk—leaving the smallest stems and leaves on the top part to act as fletching. He broke one of the canes in half, and the red milk from which the plant got its name seeped from it. Using three fingers, he then smeared his face with the bloodred war paint.

Kyle gave no warning. The first boy was approaching fast, his butterfly knife in hand. Kyle reared back and sent the javelin to him. The bloodweed stalk sailed across the bottom of the ravine making a whispering sound. His aim was true. The javelin hit the boy in his soft stomach. The tip sank in a good half inch. The boy looked down, incredulous to see the six-foot projectile sticking straight out from his body. He was even more incredulous when he pulled it out and blood blossomed like an ink spill on his shirt. He looked up at Kyle with full, murderous rage. Kyle threw again. And again, his aim was true. The boy screamed in rage and pain when the vicious point pierced his left eye. He clapped a hand to his wounded eye and ran back up the hill, bloody fluid pouring from beneath his fingers. The boy decided he'd had enough. Fate had dealt him a nasty reversal of fortune. He must tend to his wounds. The other boys scrambled behind him, and Kyle, his eyes wild and his face streaked with bloodweed gore, continued his onslaught, chasing them out of his ravine.

IT HAD TAKEN DANA A LOT LONGER TO track down Louise Edwards than she had first thought. Getting the address had been simple enough; Dana had just contacted Georgia Power. It was in a low-rent apartment complex just outside Atlanta. She followed that up by locating the DFACS worker handling Grace Edwards's case. The feeling was that Boyd Edwards had beaten his wife and sexually abused his child. In the end, Dana realized, that would explain everything. Living in an abusive household would cause the fear and introversion she had observed in Kyle. Being a witness, a powerless witness, to domestic violence and incestuous abuse, could be emotionally crippling. No wonder Kyle Edwards had looked haunted. He was.

Dana thought about the day she had followed Grace and Kyle to the little pond surrounded by weeping willow trees. She remembered how the children had held each other and cried. And Dana was angry with herself for not recognizing what she had witnessed. She could have perhaps brought an end to their abuse earlier. When she had talked to Kyle, she should have worked harder to pull it out of him. But Dana had been focused on Melodie Godwin. She had tunnel vision and did not see the true crime in front of her. The boy even had cuts on his face. It had all been right there for her to see.

None of that explained the shattered auto glass she had found along Eden Road. Or the front seat of Melodie's car adjusted for a very short person. Or the pair of boys' sneakers found in the car. The bottom line was that she still needed to talk to Kyle. She needed to be sure that she had misread the situation that, in her own blind quest for justice, she had let the boy down. And if so, she wanted to tell him that she was sorry.

Late in her shift, she had been called away to a domestic dispute that had turned into a standoff when the woman involved had locked herself into a bathroom and threatened to cut her wrists. Dana had talked the woman down, but it had taken hours. And then she had to sign the woman into the psychiatric ward at Parkway Medical Center. In the end, it had eaten up most of the night.

MRS. EDWARDS REMEMBERED DANA FROM the time she had come to her door on Eden Road. There was some level of surprise in the woman's puffy eyes, but Dana figured that with the doctors and the social workers who had just become a part of her life, Mrs. Edwards probably didn't find it too terribly odd that a sheriff's deputy wanted to check on her youngest son— to make sure the boy was all right in all of this.

"He's asleep," Louise said. "I'll have to wake him up."

"I appreciate that, ma'am. I just need to talk with him for a few minutes. In private. Just to make sure he's okay. And then I'll leave you folks in peace."

Louise went to wake Kyle, and while Dana waited, she looked around the living room. The furniture clearly came with the place. It was threadbare with little tufts of foam padding peeking out. It smelled musty and faintly of urine. Louise Edwards came back, and Dana read the alarm in her eyes.

"He's gone. He's not in his bed."

"Did he leave a note?"

"Not that I could see. Dear Lord. He's taking all this to heart. He's an emotional boy."

"I know."

"What can I do? Who should I call?"

Dana wrote a number on her notepad, tore it off, and handed it to Louise.

"I'll go look for him. If he comes back home on his own, I want you to call my station. They'll radio me and let me know. Your job is to stay here. Now I'm going to go look for him."

Dana cruised the complex. There were plenty of children and teenagers still up and about. When they saw the patrol car, they ducked into the shadows. She circled the complex twice and came back to the entrance. Ahead of her, across from the highway access ramp, a lighted plaza drew Dana's attention. The Greyhound station.

The man behind the ticket counter was a tall, skinny Nigerian with a heavily accented, high-pitched voice. He remembered Kyle quite clearly. This was a diverse area of several minorities, so a young white boy purchasing a bus ticket at night tended to stick in the memory. The man could not remember the boy's destination, but he did remember that it was within one of the local counties. Dana already knew where Kyle was heading. He was going back to Eden Road.

SHE COULD NOT SEE THE CHAIN ANY LON-
ger; her vision was mostly gone. Melodie's body had begun to shut
down.

Her fingers were raw and blistered from sawing with the slim
bit of metal. The hacksaw blade was a foot long, but only about a
half-inch wide. The metal was so thin that it bent with the slight-
est pressure. The teeth would snag on microscopic barbs in the
chain link, and her fingers would slide on the blade. She had cut
through the first side of the link yesterday, so she knew it could
be done. But she was weak. In fact, Melodie Godwin was dying.

She hadn't eaten in a week—since the boy (Kyle, his name was
Kyle) stopped coming. And prior to that, she had only been allowed a single meal each day: a pack of crackers and a can of Coke.
And the oven-like heat of the attic sapped any energy she might
have gleaned from the food. Each day it rose to at least one hundred and ten degrees. Her body no longer produced sweat. That

system had shut down some time ago. Her potty spot on the far side of the chain's perimeter held only a few rock-like stools that had hurt to pass. She had not passed urine for longer than she could remember.

The heat exhaustion, dehydration, and malnourishment had cost Melodie her eyesight. Her vision had slowly dimmed over the past few days, so that now she could only make out shadows and light.

And she had begun to have seizures.

But she sawed. It could be done. She was close. She could not see it, but by feeling it, Melodie knew that the blade had eaten more than three-quarters of the way through the second half of the chain link. It was like being in the dark again, and the Lee Dorsey song *Working in the Coal Mine* was running through her mind again. Not in a helpful or hopeful way, but in a feverish, hallucinatory dirge.

She could sense how deep the blade was set in the chain. Three-quarters through. Maybe more. But that last quarter, that last little sliver of metal was easily three more hours' worth of sawing. And her fingers were raw and cramped and she just couldn't hold the blade anymore. Bleeding where she'd snagged the crescent-shaped nail buds that were no longer growing. Her arm muscles ached. Her wrist was numb. And she was sleepy, so terribly sleepy. So very very tired.

She stopped sawing. She inspected her work, using her sore fingers to feel the groove she had cut in the metal. So close. So damn close. And there was Lee Dorsey, screaming at her about working in that coal mine and being so very, very tired.

Melodie let her fingers play across the bite in the metal. The steel was eaten almost all the way through. And Lord, she was so tired. She was slipping away. Going down.

She grasped the chain link with the thumb and forefinger of each hand and applied pressure. She felt it give a little. Then she tried again, this time calling on every little bit of strength her body had left in it.

The chain snapped.

She was free.

BUT WHAT TO DO NOW? SHE HAD GIVEN IT no thought. She had not devised an escape plan to implement once she was free of the chain. She looked out the window. Her eyesight had failed to the point that she could tell that it was dark outside, but that was all.

She had lost track of time and did not know how late it was. The window was nailed shut. Although she could no longer see it, she knew that directly below her was a green tar paper roof, most likely covering the front porch. If she could open the window, it would be an easy thing to drop to the porch roof and then to the ground. But she would have to do it as a blind woman. She would have to break the window, and she had no tools to safely do that, and the noise might draw unwelcome attention. Also, in her current physical state, Melodie realized that her legs would almost certainly give out if she tried to jump. She imagined herself lying in the front drive all night, blind and with a broken leg, naked save for her garbage bag poncho, the paralyzed man finding her there in the morning.

The paralyzed man. That was how the boy, Kyle, had referred to him, and now that was how Melodie thought of him as well. Not a monster, but a man.

There were the stairs leading down from the attic. That was her only choice. She carefully felt her way over to where she knew the stairs to be. She took a tentative step on the top riser and the dry wood creaked. Remembering lessons learned from sneaking out of her parents' house as a teenager, Melodie stepped only on the outside edges of the steps, and the creaking was no longer a problem. Her legs threatened to give out with the wide stance, but there was a handrail, and with that she was able to keep herself upright.

After fifteen minutes of slow, careful work, she made it to the bottom. She was exhausted, her body wracked with spasms. She forced herself to sit until the spasms stopped. She was scared that she might have another seizure.

The door at the bottom of the stairs creaked on its hinges. She thought of spitting on the hinges to lubricate them, but saliva was another thing her body wasn't wasting resources to produce. So she had to open it one agonizing inch at a time.

The house was quiet. There were lights on, and Melodie could make out dim shapes. Based on the position of the attic window above, she felt her way toward where she thought the front of the house would be. (If she had still had her vision, or had simply been more familiar with the layout of the house, Melodie could have taken a handful of strides to her left—slipped out the kitchen door, and made an escape that would have gone unnoticed for days. But, alas, that was not to be. Melodie went right.)

She stayed to the wall, not daring to venture out into the open space of the room and risk tripping or overturning something.

She could hear deep, rhythmic breathing. Snoring. As she worked her way along the wall, the snoring grew louder. She knew it was the paralyzed man, but she did not think that she was in his bedroom. A bedroom would be to the rear of the house.

She maneuvered past a picture hung on the wall, careful not to disturb it. The snoring was louder now, closer, and it unnerved her. She started to hurry. She just wanted out. She brushed up against a floor lamp, felt it leaning to the side, sensed it tipping over; but she reached out and caught it before it could crash to the floor.

Her hand touched a cool oval of solid metal. A doorknob. The door! She had found the door. She opened it with care, and was about to step through when the sharp odor of mothballs assaulted her nostrils. A closet. It was just a closet. She closed the door with quiet care and continued along the wall.

The snoring seemed to be all around her now, boring into her mind. She wanted just to scream, to scream and run. Her hip bumped something solid and immobile. She reached down and prodded it with her fingers. It felt like a wheel. Her fingers played upward and sunk into the flabby flesh of the paralyzed man. Melodie recoiled. The paralyzed man grunted, but the snoring continued. She stepped around him and found her way back to the wall. The hysteria was returning, and she could not stop herself from hurrying. Her hands were almost beating the wall as she rushed along it.

She jarred another picture, the cheap hook gave way, and the frame came crashing to the floor.

The wood cracked, the glass shattered.

The snoring stopped.

Melodie stood motionless in the silence. She could not even hear breathing now. She stood and listened, not daring to move. Was he awake? If he were awake, he would say something. There would be movement.

She stood in that spot until she felt her legs giving way again. She had to move or she would fall. The broken glass crackled under her bare feet, cutting them. She came to another door. It had a glass window centered high. It was the front door. She turned the knob and pulled, but the door would not budge. Was it stuck? She let go of the knob and felt along the jamb until she found the turning mechanism for the dead bolt. She retracted the metal bolt and pulled the door open.

Cool night air baptized her. She was reborn.

"Poor child."

Melodie heard the metallic click when the paralyzed man cocked the hammer of the .22 caliber revolver he kept in the side satchel of his wheelchair. There was a loud pop and the door frame exploded inches from her face, embedding splinters and shards of wood under her skin.

Melodie ran. She ran across the front porch and caught the handrail directly at hip level. Her body flipped over the railing, and she landed with a thud on her back. She turned over, gasping for breath. She could hear the electric hum of the wheelchair as it emerged onto the porch. By the time she had got back to her feet, she heard the rubber tires squeaking on the sloping zigzags of the wooden ramp.

Again, she ran. Her fall had left her disoriented, and it was purely an act of providence that she ran away from the house rather than toward it. When her feet hit the dirt road, she turned to follow its path. She was running blind. The road was her only hope.

Behind her, she could hear the electric motor whirring, high-pitched and straining now, being pushed to its limits. And over the sound of the motor, the delighted laughter of the paralyzed man. It was as if the sound of that laughter was some kind of voodoo spell, sapping the rest of her strength, her will to live. Whatever last bit of energy reserves Melodie Godwin had called upon to make her escape was depleted now. She slowed. The wheelchair was closing the gap. She stumbled like a wounded gazelle. The wheelchair was at her heels, the laughter trapped in her head.

The gunshot felt like a jabbing punch to her lower back as the .22 caliber bullet passed through her side, just missing her right kidney. She collapsed, tumbling into the roadside ditch with the last of her momentum. She was deep in weeds and brambles, looking straight up. She imagined that she could see the paralyzed man peering down at her.

"Looks like the boy will have some work to do."

She heard him grunt with exertion while he leaned over his chair to gather leaves, limbs, and trash. She felt the debris raining down on her, covering her a bit at a time. He was hiding her.

KENNY DIDN'T NEED HIS KEY TO ENTER the shed behind his house—the stupid boy never remembered to lock it. He closed the door behind him and pulled at the low hanging ball chain to turn on the light.

Kenny knew that it was only a matter of time before he was caught. How could he not be caught? The colored policewhore was so far up his ass he needed an enema to get her out. She was closing in on him and he could feel it.

He placed the pistol in his lap and maneuvered his chair over to the long utility shelf. The shelf was too tall for him to see the surface from his seated position, so he felt along the top until his fingers came to a small rectangular box. He pulled it toward him too fast, and the box of ammunition tumbled onto the floor. The .22 caliber cartridges spilled across the concrete surface. It took him several minutes of reaching and grunting to retrieve the two replacement rounds he needed.

The cartridges were hard to feed into the chamber. His hands were shaking. He needed his shot.

He needed the boy. Needed him now. He had used the boy to clean up the pets in his yard. There had been no other choice. The remains had to be disposed of, and the car hidden forever. There was no other choice. The boy was the only tool he had at his disposal. But when dawn came, it would mark the seventh day that the boy had not come to him. A solid week.

Ever since he had showed the girl what Wonder Woman was all about. Maybe he had gone too far.

And now he needed the boy again. He had to clean up the new mess.

Kenny closed his eyes and focused his mind.

He put the universe in motion and set about drawing the boy to him.

THE BUS HAD DROPPED HIM OFF TWO miles from Eden Road. In fact, not far from Melodie Godwin's home. Kyle knew where he was, and he knew how to get where he wanted to be. He walked the night. And found his way home.

Eden Road was dark and quiet, and Kyle kept to the side as he made his way down the dirt road.

He heard an owl high in a pin oak, and stopped to listen.

In the ditch at his feet, Kyle saw a faint dark movement and he could hear the rustle of a possum burrowing under the limbs and leaves, scavenging for food.

Kyle kept walking.

Heading to douglas county, dana Turpin hit the blue lights on her cruiser as she merged onto I-285, the beltway around Atlanta.

When she hit I-20, she added the siren as well.

THE BOY HAD BEEN WRONG. IT WASN'T A man. It was a monster. And she was the reticulated woman.

Her mind had again dissolved into the webwork of light and dark. But it was different this time. This time there was emotion. The webbing hummed with it. The web shook with one overriding emotion: hatred. And under the hatred, pushing it up, was the most basic of human instincts, self-preservation. The hatred would propel her to do what was necessary to save herself. The time for running had passed. Survival depended on one thing: killing the monster. She would never be free until the monster was dead.

She thought she could hear light footsteps on the road, but as she focused her hearing to listen carefully, a seizure convulsed her body. A person standing near that ditch on Eden Road would have seen nothing more than a vague shuddering movement under a dark mound of branches and leaves, as though a possum were burrowing underneath.

Five minutes later, a hand poked up through the leaves. Then another. The hands pushed away the branches, leaves, and debris. The reticulated woman sat up.

DANA KILLED THE SIREN AS SHE EXITED off the highway onto Lee Road. She kept her speed up. As she approached Eden Road, Dana flicked off the blue lights. She did not want to announce her arrival.

Eden Road was dark and deserted. There were no streetlights on this country road, and the scattered houses were mostly dark.

She crept forward, vigilant.

NEARLY BLIND, GUNSHOT, HER MIND SHAT-
tered, the reticulated woman stumbled down the middle of Eden
Road. She did not know if she was moving toward the monster's
house or away from it, but that didn't matter. All that mattered
was that she was moving. She was moving. She was going to make
something happen. Her mind called out a single message. Over
and over like a homing beacon, a single thought compelled her
onward: Kill the Monster. Her mind was not capable of forming
a thought beyond, or even in support of this one basic drive.

She stumbled forward through the darkness, and sadly, as
though fate wanted one last laugh at the expense of Melodie Godwin, she was moving away from the house of Kenny Ahearn. Her
current path would lead her to a tangle of discarded, rusty barbed
wire that Daddy-Bob had been meaning to clear out of that ditch
for years now, but never quite got around to. If Melodie had completed those last ten steps, she likely would never have gotten back
up. But before she did, Melodie paused, realizing that the dark-

ness of her world was no longer total, and she stood still, now able to make out shadows and gradations of darkness.

There was light. Coming toward her, seeking her out.

A new thought entered her mind. Hide.

Melodie reversed direction and felt her way back to her burrow of leaves and limbs. And when Dana Turpin's patrol car crept around the curve, Melodie was hidden. The light felt warm as it swept over her hiding spot. When it was past, she lifted her head and could just make out the twin red dots of taillights glowing weakly like dying embers.

The thing that was just barely Melodie Godwin crawled back into the road, and another thought filled its mind: Follow.

KYLE SLIPPED QUIETLY INTO THE PARA-
lyzed man's house. It was empty.

He had seen the light creeping through the cracks of the storage shed, but he had to be sure. Kyle searched from room to room,
but there was no sign of the man's presence. In the living room, he
saw evidence of trouble: a shattered picture, the broken doorjamb.
Satisfied that he was safe for the moment, Kyle snuck upstairs. The
attic too was empty. It still smelled of Melodie's captivity, like the
cage of a neglected and abused animal.

Kyle saw the blade on the attic floor, bent and streaked with
blood in places. He picked up the severed chain and noted where
the unoxidized metal gleamed at the cut ends. He smiled.

Downstairs in the kitchen, Kyle opened the refrigerator and
saw that the dish towel that was laid out inside to hold the prepared syringes of insulin was empty. Maybe the paralyzed man
was dead. He was capable of preparing the syringes by himself,

but only with a good bit of effort. If he had needed the insulin in a hurry . . .

Kyle dug through the kitchen cabinet and pulled out the things he would need. He sat down at the kitchen table and prepared the syringes.

"IT'S ABOUT TIME YOU GOT HERE, BOY."
Kyle watched the paralyzed man roll into the kitchen. "We got work to do, but first reach in the Frigidaire and get me my shot."

"I'm done doing for you. It's finished."

"No, son, it ain't finished. Not by a long haul. You get my shot."

"You can't make me do anything for you. Not no more. I've seen through you. You're the devil. You can't control me."

"Maybe you're right. But maybe you're wrong. The time for quittin' has come and gone. You're in this as deep as me. Maybe deeper."

Kyle stood up. "I told you I don't care no more. I'm gonna tell it. I'm gonna tell it all. I don't care what happens to me just as long as you can't hurt no more people."

Kenny picked up the pistol from his lap and pointed it at Kyle. "Sit back down, boy. You're gonna do just like I tell you." The gun shook and jittered in Kenny Ahearn's hand, and a sheen of oily sweat sprang out on his forehead. "You fix me my goddamn shot."

Kyle reached into the refrigerator and pulled out one of the syringes. Then he changed his mind and tossed it back inside, slamming the refrigerator door shut.

"Get it your own damn self."

With only one good hand, Kenny would have to put the gun down in order to open the refrigerator and administer his own injection. He locked eyes with Kyle. "You do it."

"No."

"Do it, boy. I'll put a bullet straight dead in your brain."

"No."

"I'll find your sister. I'll find your mother. I'll call them to me. I can do it. You know I can do it. Maybe you really have seen through me. Maybe you don't serve me no more, but you know I've got the power to control. Maybe you've got it too. Maybe we ain't so different."

Kyle opened the refrigerator and picked up the hypo.

"Maybe we're not."

He stabbed the short needle into the meaty thigh of the paralyzed man's dead right leg.

DANA KILLED THE ENGINE AND LIGHTS
and let the cruiser roll to a stop about fifty yards above Kenny
Ahearn's house. She approached the house with care, wary of making her presence known. A rectangle of greenish light fell through
the kitchen window onto the side yard. Dana stepped around it
and made a circuit around the house, securing the perimeter. She
checked the door to the storage shed and found it unlocked. Using
a penlight from her utility belt, she scanned the interior. She noted
nothing out of the ordinary, but as she turned to exit the building,
something small and hard like a pebble rolled under her shoe. She
shined the light down and saw .22 caliber rounds scattered across
the concrete floor. She unsnapped the safety strap on the holster
that held her service revolver.

Outside, Dana approached the lighted kitchen window from
the side. From a crouched position, she edged into the elongated
rectangle of light and peered through the window. From outside,
she would be backlit and plainly visible, but she knew that she

could not be seen from the inside due to the reflective qualities of glass.

Dana saw Kenny Ahearn and Kyle Edwards sitting at the kitchen table. The scene was almost homey, like a boy and his grandfather having a heart-to-heart. All that was missing was slices of pecan pie and glasses of milk. But then Kyle stood up, pointing his finger, and said something to the old man. The look on Kyle's face was one of defiance. Dana was so enthralled to witness the interaction between the man and the boy that she did not hear the sound of the snapping twig some distance behind her. Ahearn looked sick. His skin was pale and oily sweat glossed his forehead. He retrieved something from his lap. It was a gun. He pointed it at Kyle.

Dana stood and instinctively drew her weapon. She was going to fire. She paused only long enough to consider whether the glass pane would alter the bullet's trajectory. She couldn't put Kyle in jeopardy. She cursed herself for not having called in backup. She had to act. The sound of the snapping twigs was closer to her now, and the noise finally did penetrate to her brain. She turned to see what was rushing toward her.

Melodie Godwin, able to distinguish the outline of a form against the light, began to run toward it. The one thought now in her reticulated brain was to kill. To kill the monster. She leapt, her mouth open in a silent battle cry.

In a single fluid movement, Dana pivoted her hips, swung her arms around, and turned to face her attacker. She raised the revolver at the wraith that was coming down on her like a disease-maddened bird of prey. She fired.

"I'M STILL DIZZY. MY SUGAR'S NOT COM-ing down. Give me another one."

Kyle opened the refrigerator and pulled out another syringe.

"Do the other leg this time." Kyle complied, uncapping the needle and pulling at the top of the paralyzed man's loose fitting pants to get at the upper thigh. As he always did, Kenny averted his eyes. For while he took a certain delight in the piercing, he did not care to see the needle violate his flesh. Kyle plunged the needle in with almost tender care and depressed the plunger.

The paralyzed man cried out, "It burns! It burns!"

A gunshot exploded in the night, and the full of Kenny's attention was divided between the excruciating burning in his leg and the meaning of the gunfire just outside his window.

Kyle grabbed another syringe and stabbed it into the hand holding the pistol. The pistol fell to the floor.

Kenny pulled down the top of his pants to look at the sight of the first needlestick in his dead right leg. It had gone black. The flesh was giving off a putrid odor. Kenny prodded it with his index finger, and it sank into the liquefied flesh up to the knuckle.

Kyle scooped up a handful of the Drano-filled syringes and uncapped the needles.

DANA FIRED THE SHOT OVER THE WRAITH'S head, but that didn't stop it. As it flew through the air, the thing had its mouth open, as if in a scream, but only an airy squeak came out. It landed on top of Dana. She was able to subdue the woman easily. For it was a woman. And she had no strength, no fight left in her. Dana stroked the woman's stringy hair and soothed her, quieted her. She was Melodie Godwin. She was alive.

Dana raised her head and looked through the window. Kyle's back was to her, blocking the paralyzed man. Kyle held needles in his left hand. The syringes were interlaced between his fingers and the needles stuck out like vicious metal claws.

LATER THAT YEAR, THE COUNTRY-ROCK group Eagles would release the album *Hotel California*. From the end of 1976 and on into 1977, the eponymous single seemed to receive near constant airplay—unusual for a song of desolation and lost hope. It seemed to define whatever it was that America was feeling as it turned two hundred and then looked forward. And every time Kyle Edwards heard that song, he would think back to this night. He would listen to it, waiting for the lyrics to catch up with the tight knot he felt in the center of his stomach. Waiting for the part where the doomed guests brought out their steely knives to stab it. And knowing that they could never kill the beast.

Kyle didn't kill the beast. The paralyzed man didn't die that night. But if he ever moved again, it was upon his belly he would squirm, eating dust.

* * *

By the time Deputy Turpin took the last of the needles from him, Kyle was finished anyway. He'd prepared half a box of syringes filled to the brim with America's favorite caustic drain cleaner, and he used most all of them, injecting the Drano multiple times into Kenny Ahearn's legs and arms; and when Kyle read about it later in the papers, it said that they had to amputate all the paralyzed man's limbs. Kyle wasn't as practiced as Kenny Ahearn though, so the injection meant to burn out the man's voice box had not been clean and precise, but messy and amateurish. The acid took out the vocal cords all right, but it also destroyed the man's GI passage so that in order to keep him alive, Kenny Ahearn had to have an emergency tracheotomy so that he could breathe and, later, a feeding tube was implanted surgically to deliver nourishment.

In the few minutes they had before the ambulances and the sheriff's department got there, turning Eden Road into a dance floor of swirling lights, Dana Turpin told Kyle to walk to his father's house. She told him to sneak in it the same way he snuck out those other nights. And when he woke up in the morning, he was to say that he'd run away because he missed his daddy. That was it. No more. He would have no part in any of this. Deputy Turpin would not speak his name to anybody. In fact, Kyle would never again see Deputy Officer Dana Turpin, but thirty years later, she would call him. And when she did, she wouldn't acknowledge what had happened here this night.

Even after she recovered, Melodie Godwin also never communicated to the authorities about Kyle's role in this horror that rocked the South and reverberated across the nation. And Melodie Godwin did recover—to a degree. She did survive. Kyle read about it in the newspaper. "Lone Survivor of Eden Road Horror House Emerges." Kyle read the newspaper almost every day the rest of that year. They found more cars dumped in the reservoir. More bodies.

And with each revelation, each new obscenity revealed, the newspaper articles always included a small black-and-white photograph of Deputy Officer Dana Turpin—the source for everything that followed. It was an event that would propel her career ever forward.

Deputy Turpin reported that she was patrolling Eden Road at the end of her shift. Just watching, observing. It was a habit she'd gotten into when she first started the case, following her hunch that Ms. Godwin went missing from this lonely road. She reported that she heard a disturbance at the Ahearn residence—gunfire. She found Melodie Godwin just outside the house; and through the window, she observed Mr. Ahearn stabbing himself repeatedly with hypodermic needles.

Given the right-side paralysis of his body, there was some question as to how Ahearn could have repeatedly injected a corrosive drain cleaner into all four of his limbs (not to mention his throat). When the investigators went to pull fingerprints from the Drano bottle and the used syringes, those items had somehow disappeared from evidence. The unspoken consensus was that Melodie Godwin had in fact inflicted her own revenge on the monster, and Deputy Turpin was covering for her. The matter was not investigated any further. And if it was spoken of, it was only with a sense of regret that Melodie had been too weak and injured to finish the job.

Given the nature of his crimes, it was agreed that Kenny Ahearn was quite insane and had somehow found a way to inflict this harm upon himself.

The paralyzed man would never say any different. He couldn't.

At his trial, they carted him in on a little wheeled platform. His body was wrapped in gauze and he looked like a legless reptile. Everybody in the courtroom could hear the whistle of his breathing through the tracheotomy tube. His eyes were slitted and his tongue darted out every few seconds to wet his scaly lips.

Opal Phillips—she of the constant casseroles and longing looks—was the only witness for the defense. A character witness. For mercy. She got up on the stand and talked about what a good, kind, Christian man Kenny Ahearn was. How he was a deacon at the Lithia Springs First Baptist Church of God. She cried a great deal and slobbered on herself in a manner not unlike the fervent Preacher Seevers. Opal said that both she and God knew Kenny Ahearn was innocent of these crimes. That she would stand by him. That if they let her, she would be by his side every day for the rest of his life, ministering to him.

On his little wheeled platform, the paralyzed man rocked to and fro with such force that only his stumps stopped him from tumbling off the cart. The whistling from his trach tube grew high and urgent, like a referee calling a bad play. And tiny balls of tight white foam formed in the corners of his mouth.

MERCUROCHROME

The call from the Atlanta Homicide detective was professional and courteous.

The woman identified herself as Detective Dana Turpin, but she did not acknowledge that she had known him when he was just a boy. Yet Turpin must have sought out and volunteered for this unpleasant task—the coincidence would otherwise have been just too great.

Other than confirming his identity, there was no preamble and she flatly told Kyle that his sister was dead.

"At this time," she said, "we're deeming it an accidental over-dose."

And it was only there that Kyle felt the detective's voice belied a deeper level, an unspoken insight.

Kyle thought of the phone calls he was going to have to make. The family was scattered now, and their interactions tended to focus on holidays and funerals. But he did see them from time to time. Except for Grace, of course. He had not seen or spoken to Grace in two decades, since she ran away at the age of seventeen. No one in the family had. And if he was being honest, it had really been thirty years since he'd last seen Grace, since the summer she was seven years old.

Detective Turpin went on to sketch out a few details of Grace's final circumstances. Kyle knew the Clermont Hotel and that portion of Ponce de Leon Avenue, and he understood that this matter would not be delved into any deeper than was strictly necessary.

Voice still flat, Detective Turpin said that there was a note.

"Oh?"

"Not a suicide note," she said.

"Well, what kind of note is it?"

"It was found in her pocket, tucked inside a prescription bottle."

The detective paused, and Kyle instinctively understood that her training was to not give out too much information all at one time, to parcel it out, to see if the other party would add to it— perhaps in an incriminating way, or an exonerating way. Kyle had nothing to add, but still felt compelled to fill the uncomfortable silence.

"Really?"

"Yes. The note was addressed to you. It has your name on it."

Pause.

"My name?"

"Yes."

"Am I allowed to see it?"

"It's not a suicide note."

Pause.

"I don't understand."

"It will go in an evidence bag and be stored in the case file."

Pause.

This time Kyle didn't fill in the silence. He stood there mute, holding the cell phone to his ear.

"If you like," the detective volunteered, "I can read it to you."

"Please, yes, thank you."

"It says, 'Go to the green pond.' That mean anything to you?"

Kyle could not find the words to answer. Did that mean anything to him? It meant everything to him.

"No," he finally said. "No, that has no meaning for me. But, unless she had changed, Grace was using drugs, and had been for quite some time."

"It's sad, but, unfortunately, this kind of thing happens a lot more often than most people think."

"Yes. Thank you, Detective."

KYLE FEELS LIKE AN INTRUDER IN

the country of his childhood. A foreigner. *I do not belong here*, he thinks.

Eden Road is paved now. The cornfield has been graded and a cluster of bevel-sided split-levels has been put up (an architectural style that Kyle's wife disparagingly refers to as "double stacks"). The sweet potatoes and peanuts have been turned under and replaced with a rolling expanse of green suburban lawns. Cookie-cutter houses crowd the land that Grace and he once burned to the ground.

Their old house is still there, looking small and insignificant.

His father had lived there, alone, until a series of ministrokes erased so much of his mind that he could no longer care for himself. The silver lining of the brain damage was that Boyd Edwards no longer had to dwell on the fact that he had once been accused of molesting his daughter and that his wife had left him and married an Atlanta real estate broker.

The cow pasture is gone, replaced with a subdivision. The subdivision is recently built; many of the houses sit there unsold. Still, Kyle has to do what the note says. He has to go to the green pond. He carries a shovel with him. He explores the new subdivision, the asphalt streets and poured concrete curbs. He thinks of the old Joni Mitchell song about how they paved paradise and put up a parking lot, but this was never paradise. Maybe for a while it was. And that makes him think of another Joni Mitchell song. The one that starts off with the child of God walking along the road.

He carries the shovel with him through the subdivision. Off to one side, behind an unsold brick colonial, he sees a stand of young pine. Green and tender, no more than ten feet tall. A slat privacy fence has been built around the pines to obscure the view of what would have otherwise been an eyesore. The weeping willows have been bulldozed (their roots are bad to clog drainage and sewer systems) but he's certain this is the spot. The fence is at least two feet taller than he is, and Kyle is a big man. There is no way he can climb it. He kicks at the slats along the bottom until he finds a loose one and wedges in the shovel head. He pries two boards loose and creates an opening that he can slide through. He remembers how they used to slide under the barbed wire fence, holding the wire out of the way for one another, and he wishes Grace were here to hold the boards apart for him.

The pond is just a hollow depression now. The crackled remains of green algae cover the surface like a potter's glaze, with cattail springing up from the center of it. It remains a natural drainage spot, not fit to build on, so the developers have fenced it off. But the development of the land has altered the normal movement of rainwater, so it no longer receives enough runoff to remain a pond. It is a marshy depression in the earth, clotted with weeds.

He digs carefully, not wanting to damage whatever it is that lies beneath. He sifts through each shovelful, checking it, before scooping out more. It's nearly dark before he finds what Grace has sent him here to retrieve for her.

There is no note sending him ever onward to grander and grander adventures. What he sees is a tiny plastic hand reaching out from the dark earth—as if reaching out for help that arrives thirty years too late.

He immediately knows what it is. He's careful, like an archaeologist, as he unearths it and brushes it off. Although its features are faded and deeply soiled, he notes the costume that was once red, white, and blue, the large bust; and he can just make out the Amazonium bracelets on its wrists that can deflect bullets.

ACKNOWLEDGMENTS

I would like to thank my generous editor, Natalee Rosenstein, as well as Kaitlyn Kennedy, Robin Barletta, Jamie Snider, Tricia Callahan, Luann Reed-Siegel, and Michelle Vega at Berkley Books. I am lucky to work with these talented folks, and proud to have a home at Berkley Prime Crime.

Robert Guinsler, literary agent nonpareil, put the universe in motion and made it deliver. Thank you, Robert.

Officer Scott Luther of the Kennesaw Police Department guided me through some of the law enforcement aspects of this story. Any mistakes in that regard are mine.

Victor Daniel and Jeff Jerkins advised me on points of local geography and history, but in many instances I took liberties— particularly with the course of Sweetwater Creek as it winds its way through Cobb and Douglas Counties.

ACKNOWLEDGMENTS

Don Scarbrough and Aly Lecznar at Sweetwater Creek State Park were very helpful to me.

I am indebted to the staff and tireless volunteers of the Walken Creek Farm Literary Retreat. And my thanks to Ed Schneider and Robert Leland Taylor, whose input made this book better.

My son, Zachary, at age five, told me about The Paralyzed Man. Thanks, big guy.

And my wife, Andria, never stopped believing. Not even for a second. Her encouragement and input during the writing of this novel sustained me.